PAINTED LADY

PIPER DAVENPORT
NEW YORK TIMES & USA TODAY
BESTSELLING AUTHOR

JACK DAVENPORT
USA TODAY
BESTSELLING AUTHOR

Sale of this book without a front cover may be unauthorized. If this book is coverless, it may have been reported to the publisher as "unsold or destroyed" and neither the author nor the publisher may have received payment for it.

Painted Lady is a work of fiction. Names, characters, places, and incidents are the products of the author's imagination and are used fictitiously. Any resemblance to actual events, locales, or persons, living or dead, is entirely coincidental.

Cover Art
Jack Davenport

Published by Piper & Jack Davenport
Copyright ©2024 Trixie Publishing, Inc.
All rights reserved
Published in the United States

ISBN-13 9798317607609

Published in the United States

PAINTED LADY

Acknowledgements

<u>Liz</u>:
Thanks again. Your insight is always so spot on!

Brandy:
Thank you for keeping the characters and timelines right!
Thanks for being the greatest Ziggy EVER!

Trudy:
Thanks for your willingness to read and give feedback so quickly!

Evangeline

Several years ago…

STARED AT the Harbor Gardens sign through my windshield as I gripped the steering wheel. The last thing I wanted to do was get out of this damn car, but my therapist assured me these monthly visits with my mother were a necessary part of my recovery.

Recovery. Right.

How does one recover from what I'd been through, exactly? How could I possibly heal when my mother was there to rip open all my old wounds? So far, I was on my fifth therapist and third antidepressant, not to mention the mound of self-help and meditation books. Most of them failing to make even the slightest dent in the trauma that woman had put me through.

My mother was a monster. It's why she had been incarcerated at Harbor Gardens to begin with.

Despite its manicured grounds and beautiful, historic buildings, Harbor Gardens was a high security, assisted living facility, which meant no one got in or out without the approval and assistance of at least one security staff member. The brick building was initially designed to accommodate dementia patients with a history of wandering away from their homes and according to the brochure, 'The twenty-four-hour a day monitoring and care for its residents provides a sense of peace and security for their families.'

Eventually Harbor Gardens would partner with the Massachusetts Department of Corrections by taking in elderly, low risk, inmates in order to make room in its state penitentiaries for more 'violent offenders.'

I tried my best to ignore the implications of my mother's offenses being deemed non-violent by the court system and looked on the bright side of her transfer. Harbor Gardens was closer to my apartment than Framingham Women's Prison and a far nicer place to visit her. It wouldn't make speaking with her any less tolerable, but at least I didn't have to run the gauntlet of grabby prison guards and suffer the cat calls of the inmates telling me how they'd all love to 'make me their bitch.'

It took me another few minutes before I finally

gathered enough courage to open the door and get out. I took a deep breath, whispering, "do not take her bait," as I exhaled, before making my way down the path to the building's only public entrance. The mayflowers were in full bloom along the winding flagstone path, and I couldn't stop a smile as the small white trumpets announced the arrival of spring. My favorite time of year in New England.

"Good afternoon, Miss Evangeline," Maxine, the day shift security manager said as I entered. "How's our favorite author today?"

"Struggling writer," I corrected her. "I don't get to call myself an author until my book is finished and published, which at this rate, is never going happen."

Maxine shook her head. "No, no, no, sweetheart. You are doing God's work, which means you're using the gifts He gave to you. And if there's one thing I know for sure, it's that God's gifts are used best in conjunction with His timing," Maxine replied.

"Yeah, well. I sure hope the Almighty shows up before my landlord. My lease is up for renewal in three months and if I can't show a valid source of income, I won't qualify," I said placing my bag on the X-ray machine's conveyor belt before walking through the metal detector.

"You just send that Mr. Landlord Man over to me and I'll qualify my boot up his backside if he so much as *tries* to put you out on the street."

I laughed. "I appreciate the offer, but the last thing we need is for you to get in trouble and end up locked inside here."

"What's the difference, child? I'm here ten hours a day, six days a week as it is. Keep me out here, or lock me up with the residents, either way you know I'm gonna run the place."

"Of that, I have no doubt," I replied, picking up my bag. Maxine buzzed me in through the door leading to Wing B, and I headed down the corridor to my mother's room, pausing one last time to compose myself before opening the door.

"Look who decided to show up after all," my mother said before I could close the door behind me. "I keep forgetting the sun rises and sets according to your timing."

I glanced at the clock on the wall. "I'm sorry I'm *seven* minutes late, Mom."

"Don't you sass me, Angel."

I bristled at the sound of *that* name.

"Please, Mother, I've asked you before not to call me that."

"I've asked you before not to call me that," my mother mocked in a shrill, high-pitched voice. "You just showed up and already you're complaining."

She sat in her armchair, facing a small TV, which was turned on, but permanently on mute.

"Why don't you ever have the sound on?"

"Too much goddamned noise," she replied.

"Why don't you at least turn on the subtitles on, so you know what's happening?"

"I know what's happening," she said, pointing to the screen. "That dumbass guy is saying something stupid to that dumb bitch and now she's saying something even dumber back to him. Then at the end of the show, the bad guy gets caught, and I get to sit through commercials for booze I can't drink, cars I can't drive, and food I can't fuckin' eat. Not that you'd know anything about missing meals by the looks of you." Her eyes raked over me.

I sat my purse down on the small coffee table. "Please, Mom. I thought we might have a nice visit this time."

The rooms of Wing B, or 'residences' as Harbor Gardens called them, were essentially tiny studio apartments, equipped with just about everything except a stove. The kitchen staff prepared all meals. No exceptions. Outside food and drink had to be on Harbor Gardens' approved list. No exceptions.

"The only thing that would make it nice is if you brought me everything I asked for," she replied, pointing to my bag.

"Of course," I replied cheerily, fighting back the urge to throw the bag at her. "Let's see. First, we have your favorite. Chocolate Yum Yums."

"That's the small pack, dummy!" my mother shrieked. "Why didn't you get the big size like I told you?"

"We've been over this. Harbor Gardens doesn't allow us to bring in the large size. Only the small."

"Ah, horseshit," she replied.

I bit the inside of my lip and did my best to ignore her jabs while giving her the remainder of her care package.

She scowled as she rummaged through the pile. "That's it?"

"That's all I was allowed to bring in. Just like last

month.”

“Don’t you sass me with that lying tongue of yours. There should be twice as much food here. Maybe even more.” My mother’s mouth twisted into an evil grin, and she poked a bony finger at me. “You sat your fat ass down on your couch and stuffed your face with my food, didn’t you?”

“Mom, please.”

“Just like always, you’re a greedy piggy who takes the lion’s share for herself and leaves the scraps and bones for me like I’m some sort of damned hyena. I can see you’ve gained a few extra pounds since last time, so I know I’m not wrong.”

I’d learned to disassociate a long time ago. To disconnect my brain from the outside world while my body runs in auto pilot mode. It’s a horrible skill to have to develop but is useful in times like these.

Then, after a little less than two hours of forced small talk, micro aggressions, and plain old regular aggression, the visit with my mother came to a merciful end. Well, almost.

As I made my way to the door to leave, my mother asked something she’d never asked before.

“How’s that book of yours coming along?”

“What?” I asked, genuinely unsure of what I’d just heard.

“The book you’re writing. How’s it going?”

How the hell did she know?

I turned to face her. “Ah, fine, I guess. Good. I hope to be finished soon.”

“And it’s going to be published?” Her tone had changed. She sounded almost vulnerable, if such a thing was possible for her.

"Yes," I replied. "I signed a deal with Igloo Publishing."

"It's going to be about me, isn't it?"

"I'll see you next month, Mom," I said, before closing the door behind me. Leaving her question unanswered.

I was six years old when my mother pimped me out for the first time. The 'john' was an elderly man who lived five doors down from our apartment in Detroit, Michigan. My father had left us a year earlier and my mother was having a hard time making ends meet. I have no recollection of those times or my father. My earliest memory is of my first visit to the man who lived five doors down. That day, and every visit with him after, is burned in my mind forever.

I remember being excited because my mother gave me a brand-new dress. It was blue with white trim and had little white flowers printed on it. She told me it was a gift from a friend of ours named Mr. Earl, and that we'd be going to visit him today. I didn't know that this would be the dress I was to wear every time I visited him over the following three years.

I can clearly recall my excitement rising with each door we passed until we reached the one with the sign on it.

I began to sound out the letters. "M-A-"

"It says manager, sweetheart," my mother said.

"What's a manager, Mommy?"

"Mr. Earl is the manager of our apartment

building. That means he gets to decide who lives here and who doesn't. He's a very important man, Angel."

"And he's our friend?" I asked, beaming with pride at the idea we knew someone important.

"Yes, Angel. And do you know what? Mr. Earl says that you and Mommy can live here as long as we want to, and all he wants in return it for you to come visit him twice a week."

"What kind of visit, Mommy?" I looked up at her as we walked. "Is it a tea party?"

"Yeah, Angel. Kind of like a tea party," she said, quickly wiping away her tears.

"Why are you crying, Mommy?"

"Because I'm so happy that we get to stay here."

I climbed into my car, shaking off the memory, and taking a few calming breaths. She no longer had that hold over me. At least, that's what I kept reminding myself. Once I'd gotten my hands to stop trembling long enough to start my car, I pulled out of the parking lot and headed home.

* * *

Present Day…

My phone buzzed and I saw that it was Emory calling. "Hey, Mouse."

"Hey. I'm sorry to call so late, I know you have an early morning meeting, but we have a problem."

Emory Philips, or Mouse as I called her, was my VP of Intake and if she was calling with a problem, it was a *problem*.

I frowned, grabbing a bottle of wine and setting it on my counter. "What kind of problem?"

"Four kids are about to be brought in tonight, but we've only got one bed."

"Okay, so adjust. We've got cots and sleeping bags on the upper shelf of the supply room."

She sighed. "Madeline's here."

"Well, shit."

Madeline Andrews was our DCS point of contact, and she was a by the book kinda gal. What she really was, was a pain in my fucking ass. She pronounced her name 'Maddy-lyne' and you better say it right or you'd be corrected every time. She was never Maddy or Mad or, god forbid, Mads, if you had ten beds, you only took ten kids. No exceptions. And she made unannounced check-ins on a regular basis, and if she found more children than beds, she made a federal case about it, and we'd be reported to the health and welfare board. Or at least, she threatened to do so.

"Is she planning on staying all night?" I asked.

"She just poured herself a second cup of coffee, so who knows?"

"Holy hell, this woman is a burr in my saddle."

"Tell me about it."

"When are the kids supposed to arrive?"

"They're at Med getting checked out, and Kelly said they can be here as soon as an hour if we have room."

"We'll make room, Mouse. You just need to get Mad Maddy out of there."

Emory chuckled. "Any suggestions on how to do that?"

"Honestly? No. Try calling a fumigator or an exorcist?" I joked.

Emory outright laughed at that. "So, should I call Kelly and tell her to hold off?"

"No." I leaned forward and dropped my forehead into my palm. "Um, let me think for a second." I stared at the patterns in my marble and then sighed. "What's her favorite restaurant?"

"Huh?"

"The restaurant she bitches about not being able to get into?"

"Poisson Fantasie?"

"Yep," I confirmed. "Call Marcel and ask him if he can open a chair for her… well, for me."

"Oh, you're brilliant."

"Tell him the meal's on me, and I'll owe him one."

"Right, okay. You sure you want to do that?" Emory asked. "It's gonna cost a pretty penny."

"To save four kids? Yeah, honey, I want to do that," I said.

"Okay, it's your credit card."

"Let me know how it goes. I'll come in if I need to."

"I will," she promised, and we rang off.

I set my phone on my kitchen island and held off on pouring my glass of wine. Twenty minutes later, Emory texted to let me know Marcel came through,

Madeline was ecstatic to have a chance to eat at the famed restaurant, and we were sneaking four children through our doors in T-minus twenty-five minutes.

I finally took the time to pour a large glass in celebration.

Evangeline

I WALKED INTO the office at seven a.m. the next morning, and immediately headed to the children's wing. I was surprised to find Emory in her office and knocked on her open door, walking inside as I did. "What are you doing here so early?"

She dragged her hands down her face. "I never left."

I frowned. "Bad night?"

"Understatement of the century."

I sat in the chair across from her desk. "What happened?"

"We got a brother and sister in, Hobie and Nori,

and the brother refuses to leave his sister's side, which is fine, I get that, but the little girl keeps crawling under the bed and no one, not even her brother can get her to come out."

"Oh wow," I breathed out.

"We handed Nori a pillow and blankets, and Hobie promised to watch her, but I just couldn't leave knowing she was on a cold floor."

"I get that."

"I checked in throughout the night, but I'm pretty sure neither of them slept a wink."

I smiled gently. "I bet they're scared out of their wits. I'll go and check on them."

"Don't you have a meeting?"

"Kids are always more important," I said as I stood. "Always. You head home and take tomorrow off."

I texted my assistant to postpone my meeting as I walked down the hall, waving my security card over the panel on the wall, gaining access to the dorms in the back, and making my way to the day-room.

"Miss Evangeline!" one of the kids called and I turned to find Zoey rushing toward me.

I held my arm out to her and welcomed her hug as the twelve-year-old wrapped her arms around me. "How are you, Zoey?"

"I got an A on my math test."

I cupped her face and grinned. "I'm so proud of you! I told you you could do it."

She bobbed her head. "I studied so hard."

"Good job."

"She gets extra screen time for that," McKenna, one of our den mother's said proudly, making her way to us.

Zoey clapped. "I get to choose the movie on Friday too, right?"

McKenna nodded. "You sure do."

"Awesome." She turned and ran off to join her friends.

"She's so excited," McKenna said. "She worked so hard on that test."

"I know. Thank you for helping her with all of that."

"It was nothing. She's a pleasure."

I nodded. "She really is."

"Are you here to check on the new kids?"

"I am." I looked around. "Are they here?"

McKenna sighed. "They won't come out of the room."

We had a boys and girls dorm, however, when families come in, we tried to keep them together and since these two were particularly young, we wouldn't separate them unless they wanted to be. We had a couple of rooms that were set up nicely for siblings. They had two bedrooms separated by jack and jill bathrooms, perfect for privacy and for kids to feel safe.

"Have they eaten?"

McKenna nodded. "I took them a tray. I was just about to go and check on them."

"I'll do that. Where did you put them?"

"In seven."

I squeezed her arm. "Perfect. I'll head there

now.”

I made my way down the hall, stopping to chat with a few of the kids on the way. Once I reached Hobie and Nori’s room, I knocked on the door and then pushed it open to find a boy about eight on the bed and a little girl about six scurrying off the bed to hide under it. The food tray rattled as she kicked it in her haste to escape.

“Oh, sweetie, you don’t have to hide,” I said as I did my best to keep my distance. I sat in the chair closest to the door and smiled. “My name’s Evangeline. You’re Hobie, right?” I said to the boy.

He nodded. “Nori’s afraid, but I’m not.”

“That’s so great, honey. You’re such a good protector.” I nodded to the tray with the half-eaten food. “Did you get enough to eat? We have a room with all sorts of snacks if you want more. Or if you want something different. I can show you if you like.”

“I like bacon,” Hobie said. “Nori likes Fruit Loops.”

“Oh my gosh, I *love* Fruit Loops!” I exclaimed. “Fruit Loops are my favorite. We have some in the kitchen. I can bring you some, just say the word. And every morning we have a hot breakfast, and there’s always bacon.”

Hobie’s eyes got big. “There is?”

“Yep. Eggs, sausage, bacon, toast, cereal, including Fruit Loops.”

Nori peeked out from under the bed, the teddy bear we would have given her at intake clutched in her arms. “Can I have Fruit Loops now?” she whispered.

"Say please, Nor," Hobie bossed.

"Pwease?"

I moved to sit on the floor and smiled. "You bet. I can show you where they are. Would you like to see?"

She shook her head and slid back under the bed.

"There's too many people," Hobie said.

"Oh, I totally get that," I said. "I remember when I went to a home for the first time, it was scary."

Hobie's eyes got big. "You were in a home?"

I nodded. "Much bigger than this one. Just like you and Nori, I had been hurt and was brought to a big house and it was very scary."

"Do you live here?" Hobie asked.

"No, but I come here every day. I started this home because I wanted kids just like you and Nori to feel safe. So if you ever don't feel safe, you can tell me, okay? And if there's anything you need, you can tell me that, too."

"Wow," Hobie said.

"Would you like me to bring you some Fruit Loops, Nori?" I asked.

She peeked out from under the bed, her eyes wide as she nodded. "Yes, pwease."

"Okay. I'll be right back."

I pushed myself up off the floor and made my way down to the kitchen where I grabbed a box of cereal, some milk and a bowl and spoon. I also grabbed a few snacks I thought they might like and some chocolate milk and then walked back to their room.

This time, Nori stayed on the bed when I stepped

back inside.

"Is that chocolate milk?" Hobie asked, his voice breaking in excitement.

"It sure is." I set everything on the tray on the bed. "Do you like chocolate milk?"

"It's my favorite."

I smiled. "Well, it's a good thing we have plenty of it in the kitchen, then, huh?"

"Can I have more of it?"

"You sure can. It's all in the kitchen."

"Wow," Nori whispered.

"I'll show you when you feel up to it, okay?"

"Are we allowed to eat this?" Hobie asked.

"Yeah, buddy. You can eat all of this." I smiled. "And there's plenty more where that came from, so you don't have to worry about food, okay? You'll get lunch and dinner, too."

He met my eyes. "If it costs too much, Nori can have mine."

I bit back tears. "Oh, sweetheart, it doesn't cost too much. You can both have as much food as you need."

"Wow," Hobie said.

I smiled. "Would you like me to help you with the cereal, Nori?"

She nodded, clutching her teddy bear and I poured the cereal into the bowl, then the milk, handing everything to her, sitting back in the chair by the door while they ate.

"Have you named your teddy bears yet?" I asked the kids.

"Mine's Super Bear," Hobie said.

"Oh, that's great," I said. "Do you like superheroes?"

"Yeah," Hobie said.

"We have comic books. I'll show you where those are when you feel up to it."

Hobie glanced at Nori, then said, "Okay."

"What about you, Nori, what did you name your bear?"

Nori just shrugged.

"Well, you have plenty of time, sweetie."

She nodded and went back to her Fruit Loops. After her second bite, she said, "I'm going to name her Fruit Loop."

I chuckled. "That's the perfect name for your bear."

She grinned wide and hugged the multi-colored bear close, taking another bite of cereal while Hobie seemed to relax a little more with each passing minute.

I waited with them for the next hour and once they were done eating, Nori slid off the bed and came over and patted my knee. "Miss Evangeline?"

"Yes, baby?"

"May I have some more Fruit Loops, pwease?"

"You bet. Would you like to come and see where they're kept?"

She glanced at her brother, who gave her an encouraging nod, with a smile accentuating his chocolate milk mustache, and then she took a deep breath. "Okay."

I rose to my feet and held my hand out to her. Hobie scrambled off the bed as Nori put her tiny hand in mine and the three of us headed down the hall into the kitchen where I was able to show them where they could eat until their stomach's burst.

With the children in the capable hands of McKenna, I made a mad dash back to the offices and into the conference room. "I'm so sorry I'm late."

Skip James, my head of PR, smiled up from his seat at the head of the table. "The kids come first. Always."

I returned his smile and took my seat at the opposite head. I felt exceedingly lucky to have the team I had. Although, Emory was sitting at the table, and she should have been gone.

"Em? You were supposed to take the day off," I said.

"I will. I just want to make sure we're all on the same page before you head out on your book tour. You leave in less than a week, so you know me. All the I's dotted, etcetera."

I chuckled. "Well, I can't fault your dedication, can I?"

She let out a quiet snort. "If you did, you'd be a psychopath."

"Oh my god, *right*?" I teased. "Okay, let's get started."

* * *

One week later…

The red light on camera one began to flash, signaling our return from the commercial break and I took a deep, though imperceptible, breath and tried my best to paste on a sincere smile.

"Welcome back to the Daily with Cayley," the

show's host, Cayley Richards said, reading from the teleprompter. "We've been talking with three-time number one New York Times Bestselling author, domestic abuse advocate, and human trafficking survivor, Evangeline Monroe." Cayley turned to face me. "Thank you again for sharing your story and inspiring us all with your courage."

"It's been an honor to speak with you, everyone here, and your audience at home," I replied.

"Can you tell us a little bit about your foundation, Papillon House in Boston, and how our audience at home can help?"

"If people would like to lend a helping hand, our website has links to places that assist with victims in your local area," I said. "There is also a link to donate to our foundation, along with links to reputable non-profit organizations that your audience might like to donate in their area as well."

"Before we go, I'd like to ask one final question."

I pinched the fatty tissue between my thumb and index finger as I was wont to do when I found myself both nervous and annoyed. "Of course."

"What would you like to say to anyone watching who may be a victim of trafficking or sexual abuse?"

"First and foremost, I want to say, don't give up. Fight back every chance you get and don't stop until you're free from your abusers. Seek help from others, even if they are complete strangers. Do whatever you can to help yourself and hold on to the knowledge that things can get better." I bit the inside of my cheek. "Your life can be better."

"And what about you?" Cayley leaned in, uncomfortably close. "What do you do when times get dark. When the memories of your ordeal come back to haunt you?"

I smiled. "I'm happy to say that after a lot of work, most of the demons from my past are far behind me."

Cayley tilted her head. "And the ones that aren't?"

"I'm ready to take them on any time they want a fight," I replied to applause from the studio audience.

Cayley held up a hardcover copy of my latest book. "The title of Evangeline's book is, *Sold in Plain Sight: The Child Trafficking Epidemic in America, One Survivor's Story*. It's now available in ebook, hardback, and paperback and I highly recommend you all buy a copy and read it as soon as possible. You can find out more about Evangeline's book on the show's website. Just look for the Cayley's recommended reads page."

The show's producer gave the wrap sign.

"We'll see you all here tomorrow," Cayley said, waving to camera one. "Until then, remember that you are beautiful, and to always be beautiful to others."

After the sign off, Cayley took a few minutes to shake hands with some of the studio audience members before making her way back to me. I was still seated on the famous purple couch, a trademark of Cayley's phenomenally successful afternoon talk show.

"Thank you again for being on the show," she said, and I rose to shake her hand. "Oh, give me a hug," she said, pulling me close before I had the chance to politely decline.

I didn't like being touched against my will, and if this professional bobblehead had been paying attention to anything I'd said over the past hour she might have deduced that.

"And I promise I will read your book the first chance I get," Cayley said, before finally releasing me.

Cayley's recommended reads my ass. I doubt she's ever read anything longer than a logo on a designer handbag.

"Great," I said, once again forcing out what I hoped would be the last smile of the day.

I was only halfway through this leg of this press tour, and I was already feeling the early symptoms of 'road wear.' Two more weeks of travel and I'd be back home for eight months. The mere thought of feeling the sensation of my own bed sheets against my skin was enough to make me cry, but the overwhelming need to do my work would continue to drive me forward.

Once the Daily with Cayley taping was done, I drove my rental car back to my hotel where I quickly showered and changed before racing to the Burbank airport to catch the red eye to Nashville. I hated LA and didn't want to stay here any longer than I had to. Besides, I had work waiting for me in Nashville. Work I was very much looking forward to.

Three

Shep

I AWOKE FROM an uneasy sleep to the buzzing of my phone. I looked to see who was calling and debated sending it to voicemail, before answering.

"Hey, Armando. What's up?"

"Thank god you answered," he replied.

"Am I gonna regret pickin' up? 'Cause, this is the first day off I've had in two months."

"I hope you didn't make plans," Armando said, sheepishly.

"I regret this conversation already. The answer is no," I replied.

"C'mon, brother. I haven't even told you what

the gig is yet.”

“I don’t care. Didn’t you hear me? Two months without a break.”

“You can sleep when you’re dead. This is an easy job, and the pay is great. I promise.”

“If it’s so great, why aren’t you doing it?”

“I am. I mean, I *was*, but Carol’s sister went into labor two weeks early, so she’s gotta fly to Philly which means I gotta stay home with the kids.”

“Get a fucking babysitter.”

“You know Carol won’t allow babysitters. She barely trusts *me* with the kids.”

“So, do what all you married guys do and lie to her.”

“She’ll know, man. Carol will know I lied the second she sees my face. Then she’ll get all pissed at me and won’t have sex with me for two months which is only slightly more than we have sex now. Come on. You don’t know what it’s like being married, bro.”

I let out a low groan. “What’s the job?”

“You’re a life saver, Shep. I mean it.”

“I didn’t say I’d take it yet.”

“It’s a simple catering job for two hundred fifty people at Mandrake’s place. Buffet, no passed service. Simple, clean.”

Mandrake’s was in reference to Tobias Mandrake, a plantation owner back in the early 1800s. He had over a thousand acres near the Cumberland River which still existed, and miraculously, the family continued to own and upkeep the home. Although, in order to afford the exorbitant maintenance costs, they rented it out for weddings and events to help offset those costs. They also had a few of the outbuildings they rented out for overnight guests.

"I hate catering jobs, you know that."

"Thirty grand," Armando said.

"No shit?"

"I said you were gonna want the job, didn't I?"

"Jesus, man. You must really want to fuck your wife if you're willing to pass on that kind of money."

"Fuck you for talking about my wife like that and fuck you for also being right."

I laughed. "Alright, shoot me the details and I'll get ready."

I showered, dressed, and slammed down two cups of coffee before making sure my van was stocked with everything I'd need for the day. I then made a list of what I needed to pick up on the way, including an assistant. After a quick phone call, I managed to grab a recent culinary school graduate named Marco and swung by his place to pick him up.

"Thanks a lot for the ride," the fresh-faced assistant said as he got into the van.

"No problem," I replied. "Nancy at CHR said you're a hard worker, and I trust her word. So, unless you plan on making a liar out of sweet Nancy, I expect all will go smoothly today. Now, buckle up because I drive like a lunatic."

"Yes, Chef," Marco replied in a fresh outta culinary school, brainwashed tone of voice.

"First of all, cut that 'yes, chef' crap right now. You can call me Shep, or hey you, or whatever the hell else you wanna call me, just as long as you follow instructions and let me know that I'm heard. Got it?"

"Yes, Shep," he replied in the exact same tone.

"Good enough," I said, peeling out.

Marco immediately grabbed the 'oh, shit' handle above him as we sped down the road.

"So, when did you graduate?" I asked.

"Spring."

"Fresh outta the fuckin' oven. I'll bet you've got the student loans to prove it."

"Yeah. That's why I'm twenty-two, don't own a car, and I'm still living with my folks."

"Don't worry about it too much. Life comes at you faster and faster as time goes on. Be thankful you've got family that can provide a roof over your head and work hard to honor the sacrifices they've made for you."

"Did my dad pay you to memorize that script?" Marco joked.

I laughed. "Sorry, I'm not trying to talk down to you, believe me. I'm only thirty-five, but everyone younger than me seems like a kid."

"What year did you graduate from culinary school?"

I shook my head. "No school for me. I learned everything I needed to know inside a firehouse."

"You were a firefighter?"

I nodded. "For nine years. I was younger than you are now when I went into the academy."

"And that's how you learned to cook? Why'd you leave the fire department? Did you get all burned up and shit?"

"Nah, nothing like that. I loved being a firefighter, but I found my true calling through cooking for the house. The first lieutenant I ever served under taught me the basics of how to cook for a firehouse, and I took to it like a duck to water. Unlike most of the guys, I looked forward to my name coming up on the cooking rotation, and before too long guys were trading shifts with me. By the time I left the department I hadn't done my own laundry or scrubbed a latrine in three years. I'd use my down time to learn recipes or watch the Food Network and the crew were more than happy to let me try new dishes."

"What about technique?"

"Cooking is a lot like fucking, kid," I replied.

Marco's eyes were like saucers.

I chuckled. "I bet they never told you that at the culinary academy, did they?"

"No, Chef. I mean, Shep. I mean, no."

"You've got to look at the kitchen a lot like the bedroom. There are only so many moves one can pull in either of them. And once you master the basics, everything after that is about elevating your game. Good technique is important, but good taste is even better. You understand?"

"I think so."

"Cook from your heart, not from your head. Nobody in your dining room is going to taste how fast you chopped the onion that went into their dish."

"Okay. I can do that." He nodded. "So, the placement agency didn't have many details about today's job. I was kind of hoping you'd be able to fill me in."

"All I know is we're serving a hot buffet lunch to two-hundred-fifty people at the Mandrake House."

"Wedding?"

"No, some sort of author meet and greet thing."

"An author?" Marco asked, excitedly. "Do you know who?"

I shook my head. "Some Lady. Evangeline something. I didn't recognize her name."

"Oh, I was hoping it was someone cool like G.K. Roman."

I shrugged.

"You know, G.K. Roman," he pressed. "He wrote the Swords of Fire series."

"I think I've heard of it. Wizards and shit, right?"

Marco stared at me, his mouth agape, in stunned silence.

"Look, man. I can't remember the last time I read anything other than a cookbook," I admitted.

"They made a mega huge hit TV show out of it."

"I work for myself, which means twelve-hour days. After work, I come home, eat a bowl of cereal, and have a beer while I watch a little SportsCenter. Then it's off to bed. Wake up early and do it all again."

"Are you trying to warn me that I'll be like you some day?"

"No, kid. I'm trying to tell you that if you work really hard, and just the right amount of luck befalls you, that someday you'll *get* to be like me."

"Don't bother slowing down, I'll get out here," Marco said, pretending to open the van door.

I shook my head. "You don't have to be a grumpy loner who's married to his job like me, that's the beauty of cooking. It can take you wherever you want to go. Think of the kitchen and all its ingredients like a painter's palate. As a chef you have the freedom to "paint" whatever you want, wherever you want. You can be a line cook in a steakhouse in Manhattan, a pit master at a Texas barbecue, or a personal chef in Beverly Hills."

"Are you going to teach me how to do all of that today?" Marco asked with a grin.

"No," I replied. "I'm going to bark orders at you all day long and if you do anything wrong, I'll more than likely throw something in the general direction of your head. I'm giving you this touchy-feely pep talk so you know I'm not a complete asshole."

Once again, Marco stared in silence.

"Don't worry," I said, grabbing his shoulder. "I'm only joking. Sort of."

Marco and I pulled up to the historical home, parking in one of the vendor spots. "I'm just gonna take a look at the location and then we'll start unloading."

"I'm following your lead, Chef."

We made our way into the house and found out exactly where we needed to go, then began unloading the gear. The massive ballroom already had twenty-five tables set out with ten chairs around each and across the back wall, six eight-foot tables were set up with black tablecloths ready to house my food. Staff were moving around the space, setting our dinnerware and centerpieces, and a podium was being moved onto a stage at the front of the room. I made sure we had power, and enough room to maneuver, especially for the carving station, and then Marco and I headed out to the van to unload.

Much to my surprise and relief the day's gig went off without a hitch. The staff at the Mandrake couldn't have been more helpful, the event attendees loved the food, and Marco was proving to be one hell of a sous chef. By the time lunch service was over, the two of us were in lock step and right on schedule, giving us plenty of time to prep the desserts while the author lady did her reading, or whatever.

As lunch began to wind down a middle-aged woman took the stage and stepped up to the podium. "Good afternoon, everyone," she said, in a cheery southern drawl. "My name is Stella Banks and I serve on the board of the National Center for Missing and Exploited Children."

A warm round of applause filled the ballroom.

"On their behalf, we would like to thank you all for being here today. Without your support, we could not do what we do. Without your generous donations we would be unable to fight the forces of darkness that would see the children of our nation imprisoned and trafficked for profit. Children forced to work as private house keepers, laborers, or most commonly, as sex slaves. Our speaker today is a woman who knows all too well about this reality. She was trafficked for eleven years.”

“Holy shit, for real?” Marco whispered. “Did you know about this?”

I shook my head. Marco and I stood off to the side, putting the finishing touches on dessert, doing our best to take care of everything in relative silence.

“I am more than honored to introduce today’s keynote speaker. One of the bravest people I’ve ever met, please welcome bestselling author and activist, Evangeline Monroe.”

The room erupted in spirited applause as a stunningly beautiful woman walked onto the stage. She was tall in heels, with long honey colored hair and was without question the most gorgeous woman I’d ever seen. She took her place at the podium and waited for the applause to die down before addressing the room.

“Thank you all for such a warm welcome. I’m truly humbled and honored to have been invited here today to share my story with you. A story that, while deeply personal to me, is not an uncommon one in this country today.”

Evangeline Monroe’s voice was deep and smokey, like a cello. Beautiful and sweet even though her words were dark.

“A reported eight million children are physically exploited in this country every year. Most experts agree, however, that the number is actually between fifteen and twenty-five.”

There was something about the way she spoke

that put me on alert. Over the years as a firefighter, I'd seen countless people in all types of stressful situations and could recognize trauma-based dissociation from a mile away. Whether it be a short-term state of shock, or full-blown dissociation. Being a firefighter rarely meant getting Mr. Mittens down from a tree. Most calls meant someone's house was on fire, or Dad electrocuted himself while rigging up the Christmas lights.

For whatever reason, when it came to this woman, I could almost see her spirit leave her body as she spoke. Maybe my observations had to do with the years I spent as a first responder, or it could have just been the fact I was known to be a little more on the emotionally adept side of the male species, but when I looked at her… really studied her, she was gone. Disassociated. It was nothing anyone else would likely notice, she appeared to be engaged with the audience, would even throw in the occasional smile, but her eyes told me a different story.

She just wasn't there.

Half on autopilot myself, I handed out desserts as I continued to listen to Evangaline speak, watching intently as she continued to disappear. Every time she went into a portion of her book that was particularly disturbing, she'd fade away a little more.

The abuse this woman suffered was unconscionable, and yet, here she stood, her shoulders back, her head held high, and the beauty and strength radiating from her was awe-inspiring.

But that void. That void was concerning.

"Thank you all for listening," she said, closing her book and smiling, coming back to the present almost as quickly as she left it. "But more importantly, for hearing the plight of so many children suffering today."

The room erupted with applause and subsequent standing ovation, and then Evangeline moved around the space greeting readers and shaking hands, which I could clearly see was difficult for her. When a woman practically lunged at her to hug her, Evangeline's body locked, and I felt myself wanting to step between them. Protect Evangeline. But that wasn't my place, so I forced myself to stay put, still watching as she walked the room with a grace I'd never seen before.

"Alright, everyone," Stella said over the P.A. "We're going to take some time and let Evangeline eat, then Evangeline will sign your books in about thirty minutes. You can make your purchases by the ballroom entrance."

Stella guided Evangeline over to the buffet and I found myself standing a little straighter. Jesus, the closer the woman got to me, the more her beauty seemed to knock me out.

Her skin was like porcelain, and she was curvy in all the right places.

Fuck!

* * *

Evangeline

I was distracted as I grabbed a plate at the beginning of the buffet table. If I hadn't been starving, I would have made sure to take some private time away from everyone before mixing in, but I'd skipped breakfast and was starting to feel a little light-headed. There were just too many people around me and all I wanted to do was go back to my hotel and hide. What I wanted was to be was home, research-ing my next project.

No, that wasn't accurate.

What I *really* wanted was to feel the sting on my thigh of a project completed.

"Brisket?" a deep, molten voice interrupted my thoughts.

"I'm sorry?" I raised my head and found myself swallowing convulsively.

"Unless you don't eat meat?" the illegally gor-geous man asked, waving a hand. "We have vege-tarian and vegan options as well."

"Ah, no." I smiled. "I'm a good old-fashioned carnivore. I'll take the brisket, please."

The man grinned and I felt a zing. The kind of zing that put me on high alert.

He was tall, over six feet. He had dark hair, and a neatly trimmed beard that seemed to have flecks of gold throughout. His eyes were a piercing blue, and I could tell he was well-built under his black chef's jacket.

You may be wondering if, after years of being trafficked as a sex worker, I still felt sexual desire towards men. The answer is yes, I do. In fact, I still enjoyed sex very much. However, I had strict rules when it came to being with a man.

First, no nice guys. Nice guys were either spineless or liars and I couldn't have either. Give me a good ol' fashioned A-type asshole any day. Someone without deep feelings or much regard for anyone else. I needed a guy who thought with his dick and wouldn't have to be told how to fuck me. I knew this flew in the face of what you might hear from most women, but I'm not like most women. Sweet talk was not the way into my pants, and I wasn't looking for a relationship. I liked to fuck, and I liked to fuck hard.

"Where do you want this, Chef?" a young server asked.

The gorgeous slab of meat offering me a slab of meat nodded to the end of the table. "Next to the roasted potatoes is good."

I smiled to myself. He's a chef. Excellent. This meant he *had* to be an asshole. It's a universal truth that chefs were total pricks, right?

"How much would you like?" he asked, piercing a slice with his fork

"Um…" I hesitated, because now I wasn't sure if he was asking about the brisket or himself.

"You tell me when, ma'am," he said, sounding as sweet as can be, loading brisket onto my plate.

"That's good," I said, after he'd sliced off three pieces.

"Cornbread, ma'am?"

"Wow. You had me at brisket, but yes please. Although, you're going to have to stop calling me ma'am," I teased.

Holy hell, I was *teasing* him. Why was I teasing

him? I did not tease. Was this *flirting*? Because I absolutely did not flirt.

He chuckled. "Sorry, force of habit."

"I take it from your accent, you're a local boy," I said, unable to stop whatever it was my mouth was doing.

"Savannah, actually," he said. "But I've been in Nashville long enough to call it home." He met my eyes. "You?"

"Boston."

"Great city."

"Do you visit often?" I asked.

"Whenever I can. Best place in the world to get a lobster roll."

I raised an eyebrow. "Well, if you ever find yourself there, let me know, I'll take you to my favorite hidden gem of a restaurant. They have the best lobster rolls."

What the holy fuck am I doing?

"How long are you here in Nashville?" he asked.

"Two more days," I said.

"How about I take you out while you're here? Nashville may not be a mecca for lobster rolls, but it's a great town regardless."

"Oh, I don't—"

He slid a card out of his pocket with a gentle smile. "No pressure. If you feel like you'd like to see a little of the city, call me. My cell's on the back."

I took the card and read his name. "Shepard Waller, Private Chef."

"Everyone calls me 'Shep,'" he said.

I smiled and dropped the card into my purse. "Well, thank you, Shep. I'll see what my schedule looks like."

I went through the rest of the buffet, then Stella and I settled ourselves into a small, private room to eat and decompress before it was time for me to sign books. I had to admit, as much as the day had been a drain, meeting the handsome chef had helped ease a little of my anxiety and I couldn't quite put a pin in why, so I decided not to examine too closely. I liked the feeling of peace, and I was going to sit in that for a little while.

Clarke

*D*EEP BREATH IN *through the nose. Hold for four seconds. Exhale through the mouth for eight seconds. Repeat until the urge to wheel this goddamned infernal piece of shit machine into oncoming traffic subsides.*

I stood in front of the station house's only printer, doing my best to keep my cool as the digital display blinked ERR no matter what I tried. It was a half an hour before my meeting with the chamber of commerce and needed five copies of my report, but the printer, like everything else in this godforsaken town, was in rough shape, and decided to print one single set of documents before committing suicide. An idea I was starting to warm up to.

"Betty?" I called out to the station's elderly desk sergeant.

"Yes, Sheriff?" she replied from her desk.

"Is the printer broken again?"

"Yes, Sheriff," she replied, plainly.

I growled at the machine one last time before walking to Betty's desk. Of course, I should be addressing her as Sergeant Wolcott, but Betty insisted I call her what everyone else in town called her.

"Wasn't the computer guy just in here two days ago fixing this thing?" I asked.

Betty smiled wide. "Jerry Bellefleur. That's Jim Bellefleur's boy."

"What?" I asked, doing my best to hide my irritation.

"The 'computer guy,'" she said, using air quotes. "His name is Jerry Bellefleur."

"Why would I need to know the name of the guy who fixes our printer?"

"Seems to me a town's sheriff should know the names of as many folks as he can. Don't ya think?"

"Thank you, Betty. I'll keep that in mind. What I'd *also* like to know is when it's broken. Better yet, I'd love to know when it's going to be either permanently fixed or replaced entirely."

"Replaced?" Betty gasped. "Oh, Sheriff, we don't have that kind of money in the budget. Do you know what a new printer costs these days?"

Probably more than my annual salary.

"And we got you a new deputy like you asked,

so you can't have a new printer and a new deputy, I'm afraid."

This so-called 'deputy' was currently sitting in the conference room filling out his intake forms, considering he was fresh out of the academy. At least, that's what they told me. I don't know what academy, because I hadn't met the kid yet. I'm pretty sure he was probably someone's nephew or brother or cousin. Someone was always related to someone in this shit hole, backwoods town.

"Never mind, Betty. I'll just take these to Kinko's," I said, holding up my documents. "Where's the nearest one?"

"Nearest what now, Sheriff?"

"Kinko's," I replied.

Betty furrowed her heavily wrinkled brow. "I don't think I'd know anything about *that* sort of thing, Sheriff."

"Kinko's. It's a copy shop."

"A coffee shop?" Betty gasped, as if I'd threatened her reason for being. "Oh, no, Sheriff. I just made a fresh pot. Would you like a cup?"

"No, no, don't get up," I said, waving her off. "I need a place where I can make copies of these reports."

"They've got a copy machine in the back of the Nickle," Betty replied.

"Thank you. I'll be back soon."

"Tell Larry Walters to put it on the station's tab and if he gives you any trouble about it, you remind him that I sit next to his momma at church every Sunday. And make sure you get a receipt."

Betty's words trailed off as I exited the station house. Crossing over Maple, I headed north towards the town's largest store, the Wooden Nickle, or the 'Nickle' as the locals called it.

The Kentucky Board of Tourism's website describes Black Sheep Hollow as picturesque and serene. A delightful "postage stamp" of a town, filled with history and mystery. A wonderful place to raise a family or retire. Locals enjoy fishing, hiking, and exploring the myriad of caves and tunnels throughout the area.

Last summer, a local teen tech brainiac named Bryan Hogarth hacked into the website and changed the town's description to read.

Black Sheep Hollow aka: 'B.S. Holler' is a drilled out, dried out, fucked out, hole in the ground. A desolate 'shit stain' of a town, filled with a history of violence and racism. It's a mystery why anyone would choose to live here. A place populated by kids who didn't have a choice but to be born here, and a bunch of old fuckers waiting for their turn to die. Locals enjoy methamphetamines, huffing paint, and fucking prostitutes in the myriad of abandoned mine shafts throughout the area.

Judge Pickering gave Bryan a year of community service for that stunt. I would have given him a job. Or better yet, a couple hundred bucks and a free ride out of town. Any kid smart enough to hack into a system, virtuous enough not to cause any real harm, and bored enough to do it for the sake of a joke, shouldn't have to grow up and die in a place like Black Sheep

Hollow. It was, however, the perfect place for a disgraced, ex-NYPD detective, to live out his days in exile.

"Mornin' Sheriff Clarke," Larry Walters greeted me as I entered the Nickle.

"I appreciate you leaving the 'good' part out of that, Larry."

"Bran muffins are on aisle two if you're backed up," he replied.

"You kidding? One cup of Betty's coffee and I'm cleaned out for next two days."

Larry let out a hearty chuckle. "Ain't that the God's honest truth."

"I'm looking for a copy machine. Betty said you had one here."

He pointed to the far corner of the Nickle. "Oh, sure it's in the back. Over by the ice machine."

"Thanks, Larry," I said, walking toward the direction he was pointing.

"But it's busted."

I stopped and slowly turned to face Larry. "Lemme guess, Jerry Bellefleur is your IT guy."

Larry's face lit up. "Jim Bellefleur's boy. What a nice young man."

"Can't *wait* to see him again."

"Anything else I can do for ya Sheriff?"

Anything else? What the fuck did you do for me at all, Larry?

I forced a smile. "No, I think that'll do it. I'll just read my copy out loud to the chamber members. It'll be like story time. I'm sure they'll love it."

"Well, Sheriff. They are a bunch of cryin' babies, so perhaps they will."

My next smile was genuine. "Thank you, Larry. I needed that more than you know."

Despite my familiarity and pleasantries with the locals, I'm not exaggerating when I say my relocation to Black Sheep Hollow had led to suicidal thoughts. I loved being an NYPD detective and worked my ass off to become one. Getting kicked off the force was the greatest loss I'd ever felt, and the fact that I was fired for doing my job made that loss almost unbearable. If I had fucked up or been derelict in my duties in any way, I could understand getting canned. But my only 'offense' was investigating a man who I believed had pertinent information regarding two murder cases. Cases I believed to be connected.

* * *

Nine months ago…

I knocked on Captain Travers' office door and waited to be called in.

"Come in and take a seat, Detective," he said, pointing to the empty chair across from him. The other chair was occupied by my sergeant.

This was only the second time I'd been inside the captain's office. The other was on my first day on the job, when I was told by my sergeant that I never wanted to find myself inside this office.

"Captain Travers, sir. Sergeant Babich," I said,

taking my seat. "How can I help you today?"

"Sergeant Babich has informed me that you've been investigating Judge Faulkner," the captain said.

"That's right. I've got some very solid leads and think the judge may know something about the murders of George Hanford and Henry Duplass."

"Henry Duplass was killed in New Jersey. Well outside of our jurisdiction."

"Yes sir, but the similarities between the two murders. I mean, the two cases have to be connected."

"Do they?" Travers asked.

"Yes, sir. I believe they are, and that Judge Faulkner knows something about them."

"Sergeant Babich told me that as well. He also told me that he asked you to drop the Duplass case outright. Ordered you, in fact."

"Yes, sir, but the George Hanford murder happened in New York and if the cases are linked—"

"*If* is the operative word here. And it's a pretty big 'if,' if you ask me," Sergeant Babich said.

"That's why I've started poking around. To find *proof* of the connection between the three men. Am I missing something here? I haven't even launched a formal investigation on the judge yet."

"And you're not going too. I've known Jim Faulkner for thirty years, and the only way he could ever be connected to the George Hanford murder is if he tried the case of Hanford's killer himself."

"With all due respect, Captain—"

"Clearly, your sergeant was right about you.

You have a problem following orders. Don't you, Detective?"

"No sir," I replied, setting my gaze just to the left of the captain's eyeline.

"Good. Then it's understood that you will no longer focus on the Henry Duplass case or on Judge Faulkner?"

"Yes, sir. I understand."

"Good. Then we have nothing left to discuss. You can get back to work on the department's substantial backlog of open cases, and Sergeant Babich can reassign the Hanford case to another detective."

"What?" I challenged.

"I think I've made myself clear, Detective. We have *nothing* left to discuss. You may go now."

"Yes, sir," I said, before standing and walking out.

Later that day, the Hanford case was reassigned to Maria Esposita. She was good enough as a detective, but the real reason she was assigned to the case was because she was fucking Babich. A floor full of Detectives and these two are sneaking around like horny teenagers who think they're smarter than their parents. The whole fucking squad knew what they were up to. Esposita or not, there was no way in hell I was going to stay away from this case, or finding the connection between the two dead men and Criminal Court Judge James L. Faulkner. Captain Travers' insistence on my avoiding him only raised my suspicions. Not only about the judge, but now about my captain as well.

I needed to be very careful from then on. I would

investigate in secret, alone. Finding and processing evidence on my own. Trusting no one. That is, until I did.

As good a detective as I was, processing DNA evidence was not something I could do by myself, so when I needed a cigar butt, I'd collected from Judge Faulkner's trash can analyzed, I turned to the only lab tech I trusted, Peter Lee. For a pair of Knicks tickets, he ran the sample off hours, and off the books. However, Captain Travers must have suspected that I'd try something like this and had the IT department monitoring all lab activities. Two days after Lee ran the samples for me, I was fired and blacklisted from working in the state of New York.

Lee swore he didn't rat me out and I believed him. In fact, I think Captain Travers was tracking every move I made after our meeting. He knew damn well I wasn't gonna drop the case, and I was too determined, or stupid to prove him wrong. I didn't stop even after they took my shield. Hell, I still haven't stopped.

Evangeline

I ARRIVED BACK at my hotel and took a long, piping hot shower. It was something I did every time I was away from home. It was the last remnants of needing to feel clean on the outside when I still didn't feel clean on the inside. When I was younger, I'd give myself first-degree burns. However, after finding my own unique method of coping with trauma related stress, I'd found that I was able to lessen the heat of the water so that I was now able to cleanse my soul in other ways, so that a shower was now, more or less, a shower.

Tonight, however, it had been a little something else. A moment of pleasure. A moment of self-care.

With Shep's face in my mind as I brought myself to climax with my fingers under the water. Something I rarely did because of the shame, but something the best sexual trauma therapists encouraged in their work. Not that I'd been to a therapist in *years*. For a relationship like that to be fruitful I'd have to be open and honest, and God knows there was no way in hell that was going to happen.

Writing, and now talking about my past was one thing. I could control the narrative by choosing which parts of my story to include or omit. I learned a long time ago that the quickest way into someone's wallet was to make them feel good first. Tony Sugar, the first guy to pimp me out after my mother, used to tell me, "Always keep one hand on your john's cock, and the other on his wallet." It was a skill I learned all too well. Dealing with my reading public didn't feel much different sometimes. Tell my story, tug at the heartstrings, and they'll buy my books. It was a crass way of looking at what I did, but it's how I felt sometimes.

I wrapped myself in a robe and wandered to the windows looking over the city of Nashville. I was surprised by how tiny it was. You could walk it in less than a day. The way people talked it up, considering how much country music (and religious music) came out of here, you'd think it was huge, but it wasn't. Maybe four to six square blocks. And with Broadway being the main drag with most of the bars with live music were located, the Ryman and Country Music Hall of Fame streets were pretty much empty and easy to get to.

As I watched the lights play off the buildings, my purse seemed to beckon to me, so I pulled out Shep's card and studied it.

Should I call him?

I had two more days here and was free tomorrow. I mean, what's the worst that could happen? He changed his mind? Or we went out and had a great time? Besides, it's not like we lived anywhere near each other, so I wasn't at risk of starting anything that would require a commitment.

I took a deep breath and punched his number into my phone.

"You got Shep," he said after two rings.

"Um, hello, Shep. This is Evangeline Monroe."

"Hey there. How'd the rest of your gig go?"

I smiled. "Ah, really well, thank you for asking. I sold out of the second pressing of my book and my publisher said we're going to have to go to a third printing."

"I don't know exactly what that means, but it sounds like a good thing."

I chuckled. "It's a really good thing. My success will help a lot more children."

"Well, congratulations. That's quite an achievement."

I bit my lip, his compliment going all the way to my soul. "Thanks."

"So, do you have some time for me to take you out before you leave?"

"I really only have tomorrow night, but if you're bus—"

"Tomorrow's great," he interrupted. "Would

you like me to pick you up at your hotel, or would you feel more comfortable meeting me somewhere?"

"If you wouldn't mind picking me up, I'd appreciate that."

"I'd be happy to. Just text me the details, and I'll do that. Six work?"

"Six is great." I smiled. "I'm looking forward to it."

"Me too. I'll see you then."

"See you then."

We hung up and I texted him the hotel information, then I ordered room service and put on an old black and white movie. The perfect cap to a perfect day.

* * *

Evangeline

The next evening, Shep arrived five minutes before six and I met him in the lobby. Stepping out of the elevator, he saw me and let out a quiet whistle. "You look absolutely beautiful."

"Thank you." I blushed.

I wore a dark blue sweater dress that hugged everything, but it was extremely comfortable, and I could move in if I had to run, (not that I was anticipating the need to, of course). I also wore a pair of tall black boots that matched the ensemble with the one expensive handbag I owned. A black Louis Vuitton Never Full Tote that I'd scrimped and saved for, purchasing after finishing my first project.

"You clean up quite nicely yourself, Chef," I said.

He wore dark jeans, a pair of cowboy boots that were obviously worn but well maintained, and a blue button down that matched his eyes. Lordy, he was gorgeous.

"Thank you," Shep said with a chuckle. "My truck's out front. Are you still comfortable going with me?"

"I'm good."

We walked out to the front and Shep held the door for me, but he didn't touch me. Something I both appreciated and hated. He was obviously giving me space but for whatever reason, he was someone I would have welcomed some kind of physical touch from.

Shep met my eyes. "I'd like to take you someplace special, but I need you to swear to secrecy first."

I laughed. "Oh, wow. Now *that* is a good line. I have to admit I've never heard that one before."

"No, I'm serious. If I promise to show you something really cool, can I trust you not to tell anyone about it?"

"Yes." I smiled. "You can trust me to keep a secret."

He closed my door then climbed into the truck, and we headed out into the countryside of Tennessee, weaving through some of the most gorgeous scenery I'd ever experienced. Twenty minutes later, five of which were spent traveling up a private tree-lined road, we arrived at what I could only describe as a grand estate. The house stood three stories high, and was surrounded by sprawling gardens, all of which were immaculately groomed.

"What is this place?" I asked, leaning forward to peer through the windshield.

"This belongs to a client of mine," Shep replied, casually, as we rounded the large circular driveway, parking at the top. "I've cooked for him and his guests many times over the years."

"You know the guy who lives here?"

"Technically, he lives in New York, and he's got other places around the world, but *this* is the house he brings people to when he wants to impress them."

"Is that why you've brought me here?" I raised an eyebrow. "To impress me?"

Shep shook his head as he pulled the truck into the circular driveway and parked. "I brought you here to give you a meaningful experience that will blow your mind and stay with you for as long as you live."

Something about the sincerity in Shep's voice caused a shiver to run down my spine. "Wow. What could possibly be inside that house that could live up to that kind of hype?"

Shep grinned, turning off the engine. "Come with me and I'll show you."

We got out of the truck and made our way to the front entrance, the large wooden doors opening for us before we even had the chance to knock.

"Good evening, Mr. Waller," said a uniformed butler as we entered.

"How you doing, Graham?"

"Fine, sir, thank you so much for asking," the butler replied in a distinguished British accent which made him sound like a character sent straight from central casting.

"How's that new hip of Alice's treating her?"

Graham sighed, before grimly replying, "She's enrolled us in a ballroom dancing class."

"Sounds like the surgery was success."

"Apparently, you've never taken a ballroom dancing class before, sir," Graham said with a soft chuckle before turning his attention to me. "And who is this enchanting young woman you've brought with you tonight?"

"This is Ms. Evangeline Monroe."

"Hello," I replied, unsure of whether I should bow or curtsy. This whole encounter seemed so fancy and formal. In the end, I decided on a hand-shake, which Graham graciously accepted.

"I take it you're here to see—"

Shep waved Graham off. "Shhhh, no, no, no. I want Evangeline to be surprised."

"I understand, sir," he replied with a knowing smile. "I took the liberty of setting out some re-freshments for you downstairs. Please let me know if something isn't to your liking or if you should re-quire anything more."

"Thank you so much, Graham. I'm sure it'll all be perfect," Shep replied.

"You know how to contact me should you need

anything," Graham said, before turning and leaving us.

"What is all this?" I asked. "Why does the butler know you so well. How many women have you brought here? Why does this place even have a butler anyway if no one is living here?"

"I've never brought anyone here before tonight," Shep replied.

Another shiver.

Shep smiled. "But I have come here often enough to get to know Graham and some of the other staff members."

"This place has a staff?"

"It's got a whole lot more than that. Come on," he said before holding out his hand, which I took without a second thought, suddenly realizing that I'd never willingly held the hand of a man. For all of the ways men had touched me or made me touch them, I'd never known the simple, innocent pleasure of holding hands. Something about Shep made me want to trust him, and while the idea of putting any amount of trust into a relative stranger scared the shit out of me, my fear was unable to override the peace I felt whenever I was in Shep's presence.

As he led us through the house, I was gobsmacked by what I saw. Every piece of furniture looked to be an antique, some of them quite rare. On every wall hung beautiful masterpieces, one located at the top of a spiral staircase which led to the lower level, stopped me dead in my tracks.

"Is this a real Rothko?" I asked in stunned disbelief as I stood before a painting I'd only ever seen in books and on the internet.

"I'm not sure. If Rothko's painting are expensive, then my guess would be yes. The place is filled with uber rich guy shit."

"This piece was sold at auction in 2012 for forty-three point two million dollars," I said, still in shock that I was standing six inches away from a true masterpiece. No glass dividing us. No velvet rope or security guard from keeping me from reaching out and touching it.

Shep let out a low whistle. "That's a lot of cheddar for one painting."

"It's not even one of his top ten most valuable paintings."

"How do you know so much about art?"

"If I'm curious about something, I tend to study it very closely. When I go down a rabbit hole or begin a new project, I do every bit of research I can on the subject."

"A self-educated woman," Shep said.

"I still can't believe this painting is just hanging on a wall at the top of a staircase right in front of me. Why isn't this house locked down like a fortress and why is the butler letting us mosey around the place unaccompanied?"

"Oh, this place *is* like a fortress. There are hidden cameras everywhere, plus sensors, motion detectors, and a security team that monitors it all twenty-four-seven. As for why Graham let us in, in short, his boss trusts me."

"And why exactly would a multi-gazillionaire trust a chef to that extent?"

"First of all, offense taken," Shep said with a smile. "Why he trusts me is between him and me, but I will say that when you cook for someone long enough, you get to know them at a very intimate level. I've cooked and shared many meals with the owner of this house. He trusts me because I've never given him a single reason not to."

"Okay, enough suspense. What's this totally mind-blowing thing you want to show me?"

"Not a thing," Shep corrected. "A who."

"You're going to show me a mind-blowing who?"

Shep grinned wide. "Exactly. Come on. Follow me downstairs."

As we made our way down the staircase, I began to see flickers of light dancing on the woodwork which grew in intensity as we descended. I'm not sure what I was expecting to see downstairs, but I can safely say what I saw next came as a complete surprise. The house's lower level was a huge dug-out superstructure made of concrete and steel. Except for the back wall, which was made of thick glass. Behind that glass was a huge water tank which contained two live dolphins.

My jaw dropped and tears immediately began to flood my eyes. "Are th…those real?" I asked. Even more stunned by the dolphins than I was the Rothko.

"Evangeline Monroe, may I introduce you to Fred and Ginger."

The pair of dolphins began to swim in tight circles and loops that almost seemed coordinated, as if on cue.

"Oh, my god. They are magnificent. What are they doing…I mean…how…how are they here?"

"The guy who owns the house rescued them from a defunct water park in Singapore. Unfortunately, since they were born in captivity, it's unlikely they can ever be released back into the wild, so he had a massive salt-water tank built to house them. It's as tall as the second story and almost as deep underground. The top of the tank is exposed to the sky but isn't visible from the outside due to how it was constructed."

"You were right. I can barely believe what I'm seeing."

Fred and Ginger continued to show off for us. Blowing bubbles and "dancing" around the tank. Giving us our own private show.

"Do you want to meet them face to face?"

"Can we?"

Shep nodded with a grin. "Follow me."

We walked up a flight of stairs and into a locker room of sorts.

"Go ahead and switch your boots with these," he said, handing me a pair of rubber goloshes. "They should fit."

Once I swapped footwear, he handed me a large, yellow rain jacket and I slid it over my dress, then laughed. "I look like I should be on a box of frozen fish sticks."

"Trust the Gorton's Fisherman," he sang, off-key, then cleared his throat. "As you can see, I'm obviously not in Nashville for a singing career."

I raised my hands in surrender. "I wasn't going to say it."

He grinned, sliding on his own rain slicker, then guiding me out another door that led us to where Fred and Ginger were more accessible.

"Hey, man," a deep voice sounded from my right, and I couldn't stop myself from stepping closer to Shep.

Shep stepped slightly in front of me and held his hand out to the man. "Hey, Terry, how are you? This is Evangeline Monroe. She's my guest tonight and I wanted to introduce her to Fred and Ginger." He stayed between me and Terry, so I didn't have to shake the man's hand, doing it with such ease, it didn't seem weird that I didn't. "Evangeline, Terry's the dolphins' handler. He makes sure they're well taken care of. He's been with them almost since the beginning."

Before I could say anything to Terry, one of the dolphins let out a little cackle and spit water all over us.

"Ginger!" Terry admonished.

I couldn't stop a snort-laugh as I turned to face the tank and watched as Ginger used her tail to dance backward in the air. "Now I see why I needed to change."

"Shit, sorry," Shep said. "I didn't think she'd come in so hot."

"Don't worry about it," I said. "She's just playing and that was kind of fun."

For the next twenty minutes, Terry showed us a few 'tricks' the dolphins could do, but for the most part, we just hung out with Fred and Ginger, and I even got to pet their noses. They were the coolest things on the planet.

Terry took a call from the phone on the wall and let us know dinner was ready, so we said goodbye to our dolphin friends, headed back inside to change into our regular shoes. We then made our way down to where we could still see the tank, but now a table had been set up with a candlelight dinner for two.

"Oh, wow," I breathed out. "This is beautiful."

Shep held my chair and waited for me to be seated before asking if I'd like wine, and when I said yes, he poured before sitting in his own chair.

"Wait a minute." I cocked my head. "You're not going to tell me *you* own this place, are you?"

Shep laughed. "I'm a regular Bruce Wayne."

"Fighting hunger by day, billionaire playboy by night?"

"Still working out my superhero schedule," he retorted. "But no, I don't own it. I wouldn't know the first thing to do with all this money."

"Well, dolphin rescue seems like a good place to start."

"Yeah, I give Gunnach points for style on that one."

My eyes widened. "One of the Gunnach's owns this house?"

"Oh, shit, you're gonna need to forget I said that," he hissed.

"Your secrets are safe with me."

"Damn I haven't even had any wine yet. I guess I just feel so comfortable around you, I forgot to keep my big damn trap shut."

I smiled, butterflies forming in my stomach. Comfortable, indeed.

It was an alien emotion to me when it came to men who seemed kind. Kind, soft-spoken men had always done the worst damage, but there was something about Shepard Waller that put me at ease, and I wasn't sure if that should set off alarm bells or not.

I was banking on him being on his best behavior because he had to bring out the chef asshole at some point, right? Otherwise, this would never work.

For now, I was going to do my best to relax and enjoy the moment. The wine was good, the food superb, and the company absolute eye-candy. What more could a girl want?

Evangeline

I GOT AN early start the last day of my Nashville stay. It would take me over two hours to drive to the warehouse from the hotel, and I wanted to get there before dark. I had a feeling I'd be working late and needed to make sure I left myself enough time to clean up and close shop before I flew back to Boston.

I found the variety of commercial spaces available in a place like Nashville to be extremely convenient. There were obviously plenty of garages, long term storage lockers, and the like in Boston, but I never worked from home. It was one of my steadfast rules. Even if I should come across a potential client at the corner market, there was no working in Boston. I tried to avoid Massachusetts entirely, if possible.

Unfortunately, I've had to work in the state twice. Both times were unavoidable.

Traffic out of the city center wasn't too bad and I made it to the warehouse in record time. Craig's Self-Service Storage and Repair wasn't the best place in town. It wasn't even the cheapest. It was, however, remote, payable by cash, free of security cameras, and private. In fact, the whole time I'd been there, I'd never seen another customer or staff member on the premises. In truth, Craig's was a front for a small-time criminal organization run by two Russian brothers, Boris and Ivan Vasili.

They smuggled black market goods out of the gulf states to Russia three or four times a year, and I was well acquainted with their shipping schedules and cargo manifests. Of course, they didn't have a clue that I knew any of this, and as long as the brothers never moved girls, I had no intention of getting in the way of their business. All I needed was a suitable workspace and absolute privacy, and Craig's provided both. By now, I had spots like this set up around the country. Out of the way, non-descript, workspaces, where I could be left alone to my work. My art. My therapy. Last night I dropped off my cash payment in the office lock box slot as usual, along with my tools and canvas, which I locked up in my assigned bay.

I pulled the rental car into bay number five, at the far end of the complex, and parked as close to the exit as possible. If someone was to show up un-expectedly, I wanted the quickest path out of here.

Plus, the further away I parked from the workspace, the less chance of getting anything on the car while I worked.

I did a thorough check of the property and verified that I was the only paying occupant of Craig's. In fact, according to the private and secured company calendar I had no problem accessing, I'd have the place to myself all week if needed. I wouldn't, of course, but loved the idea of taking an entire week to work on one project. The idea seemed like a luxury but in truth I didn't think I'd have the kind of restraint needed to wait a whole week to bring a piece to its conclusion. This one I'd been researching for over two months, and I couldn't wait to get started. This one was an especially personal undertaking, and my head was buzzing with new ideas.

Crossing the shop floor, I made my way to the only enclosed room in the space. A ten-by-ten-foot room with a window overlooking the shop. Inside the room was a metal office desk, and a row of three upright lockers where I'd stowed my gear and canvas. I dialed the combination on the pad lock securing the first locker, removing my toolkit, and setting it on top of the desk, pausing before opening the second locker.

I pressed my ear against the sheet metal door, listening for signs of life of Craig's Self-Service Storage and Repair only other current occupant.

The occupant of locker number two was my guest. His name was Barry Holland and until last night, I hadn't seen or spoken to him in over a decade. In fact, he didn't recognize me at all when I approached him at the Hotel Garmond bar and asked if he needed *company* for the night. I didn't fault him for not recognizing me. After all, I *was* wearing a disguise, and it had been so long since he'd last seen me.

"Thank you, but I'm married," he said, tapping his chubby, ringed finger against the side of his glass.

"So are most of my clients," I replied.

He chuckled softly. "I'll bet that's true."

"Can you at least buy a lady a drink?"

"Now you're in luck, because I hate to drink alone and I happen to love redheads" he replied, flagging the bar waitress who came directly to our table.

"Yes, sir. May I get something for either of you?"

"Another Macallan eighteen for me please," Barry replied.

"I'll have the same," I said.

Barry tipped his nearly empty glass to me. "A woman of taste, I see."

"When a man of taste is buying," I replied. I told him my name was Chloe, and that this hotel bar was my favorite place to connect with potential clients, as I always found them to be what I considered high caliber men. The truth was I was only here because this is the hotel Barry checked into. I also knew from experience, that as long as I stroked his ego, Barry would remain a captive audience. Soon he would simply be my captive.

Barry smiled and introduced himself. He told me he was travelling on business, which was true, and that he was in the luxury car trade, which was a lie. He also told me he lived in Miami, but of course I knew that in truth, Barry Holland was a sales representative for Duplass Modular Sheds in Sandusky, Ohio. He was married with two children and held roughly sixty-three thousand dollars in credit card debt. His wife, Sheila, was a junior-high school vice principal, and unbeknownst to her husband, had twelve thousand dollars of her own money socked away in a private savings account. She'd also been fucking the art teacher at her school for the past nine months. Something else Barry didn't know about.

I knew because I always did my homework. Every project started with a thorough and comprehensive investigation. Lucky for me, locating and investigating subjects is easier than ever before thanks to social media profiles, weak passwords, and everything from personal calendars to financial records being stored on the cloud.

"Personally I'd take the Audi RS Q8 over the Mercedies 300 SLR every day of the week," Barry said, droning on, trying to impress me with his knowledge of high end cars.

I acted like I was taking in his every word, making sure to stroke his ego every change I got. I knew full well that Barry would never take the bait I was dangling in front of him, as I was way too old for him, but I didn't need him to. All I needed was for him to relax and drop his guard long enough for me to drug him, and for everyone in the bar to believe Barry was just some drunk businessman chatting with a hotel bar hooker. That way, no one would think twice when we left together, even if Barry's steps might be a bit wobbly.

"Oh, no," I said, interrupting Barry's fascinating lecture on torque ratios.

"What is it darlin'?"

"I forgot to ask the waitress for a cherry."

"I don't see her anywhere," Barry said, craning his neck to look for her. Of course, I'd waited until I saw her leave the area before I made my 'discovery.'

"Can you be a doll and get me a cherry from bar?" I asked.

"It would be my pleasure, Miss Chloe," he replied.

As soon as he was out of sight, I opened the vile of tranquilizer I had in my pocket and emptied it into Barry's drink. I'd experimented with several drugs over the years and eventually landed on a mixture of Midazolam, Rohypnol, and Ketamine that I'd dubbed "Nightfall." I needed my subjects to be highly suggestable, completely at ease with me, and able to move around without much assistance. I was five foot, seven inches tall and weighed one-hundred-twenty-five pounds and couldn't move a full-grown man around all by myself.

"I got you two," Barry said, returning to the table dangling two maraschinos by their stems.

"You're so sweet," I said, smiling as wide as possible.

Barry sat back down, and we continued our conversation as we finished our drinks.

"Careful," Barry said, pointing to my glass. "This stuff packs a punch."

"Feeling pretty good, huh?" I asked innocently.

Barry tugged at his shirt collar before loosening his tie. "To be honest, I'm feeling kind of hot."

"Let's step outside for a few minutes. You can get some air while I have a puff." I pulled a vape pen from my pocket and wiggled it in front of him. "Besides, I'll feel much safer if you're standing out there with me."

"Sure, sounds good," Barry replied.

"I'll just let the waitress know that we're not skipping out," I said. "I'll meet you outside."

Barry nodded and headed for the exit, and I tracked down our waitress.

"Hi," I said. "My date and I are going to take a little stroll through the Park. He asked if you could please charge our drinks to his room."

"Of course, ma'am," she said.

"And he said this is for you," I said, giving her a crisp one-hundred-dollar bill.

The waitress smiled and gave me a slight bow. "I hope the two of you have a wonderful evening."

"I will, anyway," I retorted, and walked out the door.

I opened the locker to find Barry just as I'd left him. Naked, gagged, and cuffed around his wrists and ankles. I'd also secured a shock collar around his neck, a device of my own making, constructed from an S&M bondage collar and two military grade stun guns. It was my way of keeping a subject quiet in my absence. The amped up 'bark collar' was powered by a car battery which I'd fitted with an automatic potentiometer. If the wearer of the collar attempted to make a sound, they would receive a highly painful and nearly fatal shock. With each subsequent sound, the amperage delivered would increase slowly but noticeably. So far, no one had pushed the collar to the fatal limit, but I'd bet some wished they had.

"So, how was your day?" I asked in a sing-song tone.

Barry looked like a giant lump of chewing gum, crammed inside the locker. He was hunched over, with his face pressed against one side of the cramped space. He was dripping with sweat, standing in a puddle of his own piss.

I opened my tool kit and took out my gun, a Baretta 9mm compact, pointing it at Barry's head. "Here's what's going to happen. I'm going to uncuff your ankles and take the collar off you. Then you're gonna step slowly out of the locker and walk out to the shop. Do *anything* I don't like, and I will shoot you in the balls, then in the face, in that order. Do you understand?"

Barry nodded, so I unlocked the collar, letting it drop to the floor, before uncuffing one ankle.

"Okay, now step out slowly," I said, keeping my gun trained on him.

Barry took one uneasy step outside the locker

before falling, face down onto the cement floor, whimpering in pain as his body connected with the concrete.

I let out a quiet tsk. "Looks like your legs fell asleep there, big boy. That's okay. We'll wait a few minutes to get the blood flowing again before we proceed. I'd hate for you to develop a blood clot. Those things can kill you, ya know?" I slung the toolkit over my shoulder.

Barry writhed on the floor, desperately trying to talk, but only able to produce muffled screams.

"I feel like you want to tell me something," I said to a series of excited groans and grunts. "If I remove your gag, do you promise not to yell?"

Barry nodded.

"Good, because it's pointless. No one is here to save you, and I hate listening to grown men cry."

I pressed the barrel of the Baretta into Barry's temple with my right hand, while removing his gag with the other.

"Please don't kill me," he begged through gasps and chokes.

"Who said anything about killing you?" I asked, innocently.

"Please," he continued. "I have money. I can pay you whatever you want."

"Oh, Barry, please don't embarrass yourself. We both know you're a middle-class, suburban jackass with a mountain of credit card debt and a refinanced house that's twenty years from being paid off. Your kids have more tooth fairy money than you have in the bank."

"H…how…how do you know that, and w…what do you want from me?"

I stood up and waved the gun toward the door. "Your legs should be working good enough by now. Get up and walk out to the shop."

"Who are you?"

"I'm the woman who's going to put a bullet in your tiny nut sack if you don't get up and walk."

Barry got to his feet, and we made our way to the shop floor. In the center of the space was a hydraulic engine hoist, from which hung a heavy iron chain with a hook on the end.

"Raise your arms," I ordered.

"Please, you don't have to do this," Barry whined.

I dug the barrel of my gun into his temple. "Raise your arms and hook them up."

Once he'd done as instructed, I made my way to the hoist's control panel, powered it up, and using the joystick, raised Barry about a foot off the ground, causing him to cry out in pain as his arms threatened to leave their sockets.

"That's better," I taunted. "Dangling on the end of a hook, like the worm you are."

"What do you want from me? Please tell me and I swear I'll give it to you," Barry begged through sobs.

"I know you will," I said, wheeling the shop's large industrial step ladder into place beside him. "Because the only thing I want from you is your suffering."

Barry's sobs turned to blubbering. "Why are you

doing this?"

"I'd save my tears if I were you. They don't have any effect on me, and you're gonna need them more later. Because whatever pain and fear you're feeling is nothing compared to what's coming. This here, right now is as good as it gets for you, Barry. You and I have a long night ahead of us. An awfully long night."

Barry wriggled and jerked his body to no avail. "Who are you and why are you doing this?"

"I'm doing this because you pay to have sex with underaged girls. You rape children, Barry."

"I don't know what you're talking about. You have the wrong guy."

"Lie all you want. It makes no difference. We both know the truth about who you are and what you do. Besides, I never forget a man once he's been inside me."

Tears streamed down Barry's face. "I swear to god if you let me go, I'll turn myself in to the police. Or you can turn me in yourself. Just don't hurt me."

I laughed. "Does this seem like a law-and-order type of situation to you? If I wanted you inside a jail cell you'd be in one. No, you're right where I want you. As to my identity, my name is Evangeline Monroe, but you knew me as Angel."

I removed my red wig and let fall onto the tarp I'd laid out on the floor.

Barry squinted. "Angel?"

"That's right."

He shook his head vigorously, his jowls flapping violently. "No, no. You have the wrong guy. I don't know you, after all. I don't know anyone named Angel."

"You knew me when I was fourteen years old, you piece of shit. I was one of Tony Sugar's girls. Back in Detroit."

Barry's eyes widened.

I climbed the step ladder so that I was eye level with Barry. "You remember me and I sure as hell remember you."

"I'm sorry. I…I…I'm so sorry. That's not who I am now. I swear!" Barry groveled. "I have a family."

"A family who'll be much better off without a pedophile like you in it."

"I promise, I've changed. I swear to you."

"Men like you are incapable of change," I replied. "So, save your breath for screaming. Besides, this isn't a trial, it's judgement night. Tonight, the scales of justice will be balanced."

"I'm begging you. Please don't make my wife a widow. If you let me go, I swear I'll pay you whatever you ask. I'll find a way."

"My scales aren't balanced with money, Barry. They're balanced with flesh. You partook in my flesh all those years ago, so now I'm going to partake in yours. You must admit, it's only fair."

Barry continued to thrash and wriggle, screaming out for help in vain.

"You're exactly as I remember you," I said, staring into his bloodshot eyes. "You were a self-important blowhard then as much as you are now. A gluttonous pig of a man, who's in love with the sound of his own voice. A child rapist and torturer.”

“Now, now, now, wait a minute. I n…never raped or tortured anyone. I paid for sex, that’s all.”

“You paid to have sex with children. Children who were delivered to you against their will. Children who were beaten, drugged, and gang raped into submission so sick bastards like you can do whatever you want with us.”

“I’m sorry,” Barry cried.

I shook my head. “You’re not sorry. Not yet.”

I rolled out my toolkit on the top platform of the ladder. Removing a pair of tin snips from their designated pocket.

“Once a month for almost two years, Tony sent me to your room at the Royal Harbor Motel. Inside that room you proceeded to stick your pathetic little dick in every one of my “sweet little holes” as you were so fond of saying. But that wasn’t the worst of it. No, the thing I remember the most about our little visits was how you’d force me to suck on your toes while you jerked yourself off. I remember it was the only way you could come. Every time you’d put your disgusting sausage toes in my mouth, it took every ounce of strength I had not to bite them off. Well, not anymore.” I raised the tin snips to his eyes.

“Oh, god. No.”

I smiled wide. “Tonight, you’re gonna find out how much fun it is to have your toes inside your mouth. Hold on, I’ll be right back.”

Barry continued to thrash around as I made my way back down the ladder, begging and pleading for me to stop. Unable to comprehend the absolute futility of his words. Bargaining with me as if I were human. But he, and all the others like him, had turned me into something inhuman a long time ago. Now all I lived for was my work.

For justice.

Vengeance.

I started with his left pinky toe.

Snip.

Evangeline

"WE'RE SO SORRY, Evangeline, it's just not safe to travel," my agent said. "Hurricane warnings are happening all over the area, so we're going to postpone the Savannah signing until we get the all-clear sign."

"You don't think we'll have to cancel, do you?

"So far, we're only looking at a postponement, and we've got some time to play with before your next stop."

"I understand," I said with a sigh. "So, what does this mean for now? Do I go home?"

"Would you mind staying put? We're hoping the weather will clear in a few days, and we'll cover the hotel until it does. Go out to dinner, on me. Enjoy everything Nashville has to offer. If we can't get the event rescheduled for Thursday, we'll call it and send you home."

I bit my lip. It was risky, staying in town for so long after finishing a project. Now that Barry was off my to-do list, I was anxious to get my next project underway. The next one was going to be rather… well, satisfying, as he'd been hard to track down. Creepy little bastard.

But a little more time with Shep? Now that could be nice.

"Sounds good, just keep me posted and I'll sit tight until I hear from you."

After finishing up the conversation with my agent I opened the bottle of wine I'd selected for the occasion and grabbed my kit from the bottom drawer. After opening the bottle and pouring myself a hotel room plastic cup full of wine, I prepared a workspace on top of the bed, unpacking my tattoo machine.

Gloving up and sterilizing the equipment, I prepared a needle by giving it a slight bend for better skin contact at the angle I'd be working from. Then I wrapped and banded the machine, connected the power supply and footswitch before loading the machine with ink and was finally ready to begin.

Sitting up straight on the bed, I relaxed my thighs until I was in a comfortable position. Once I started, I didn't want to stop until I was completely finished. Then I started the outline of butterfly number seven. The needle delivering its first delicious sting.

As a teenager I started cutting as a coping mechanism for my trauma. Small razorblade cuts on my inner thigh. Self-inflicted, controlled pain to drive out the demons of victimization. Most of the cuts healed without scarring, but a few times I cut too deep. After my mother's death I had one of the scars covered with my first tattoo. A monarch butterfly. Its glorious wings spread in flight. And as I lay in that tattoo shop chair, lost in a haze of revelatory pain, I had a moment of clarity. A vision of my future. An understanding of exactly who I was and what I was to do with my life. The ones who had abused me had called me 'Angel,' and now I would revisit them all as the Angel of Death.

* * *

Clarke

I poured my third glass of Scotch, slowly swiveling back and forth in my chair, while studying the evidence board I'd tacked up on the wall. I'd transitioned my living room into a makeshift squad room long ago. I didn't own a TV and never had guests over, so I figured why not use the space for something constructive.

Dating in the Holler was an absolute no-go, for many obvious reasons, and if I ever did meet a woman I wanted to screw, I'd pay for a room at the Night Owl Inn. Besides, it wasn't like I could use the actual police station house, of which I was Sheriff, to do important police work. This investigation was strictly off-book, and I was on my own when it came to collecting and examining evidence. Once I knew the identity of the killer and how his victims were connected, I could go straight to the FBI. Fuck Captain Travers and Sergeant Babich and the goddamned NYPD for that matter. I was going to use solving this case as my resume for a new career with the feds. Between my position as sheriff and the various law enforcement connections I still had, I was able to poke around and collect evidence fairly inconspicuously, and felt I was on the verge of a major breakthrough.

At the center of my evidence board were pictures of George Hanford, a New York financial advisor, and Henry Duplass, Vice President of FarmTown Foods in Baltimore, Maryland, who was murdered while on a business trip in Newark. Both men were found dead within four days of one another. Both had been tortured and disfigured prior to death but were ultimately killed by a single gunshot to the back of the head. Their corpses dismembered and dumped out in the open. Despite the similarities and proximity of the two cases, early investigations found no link whatsoever between the two men. To the knowledge of both the NYPD and NJPD, the two had never met, nor did they run in the same social, religious, or work circles. Forensic testing proved that a different gun was used in each of the killings. One a .22 caliber handgun was used in the Hanford killing, while Duplass was shot with a .38. Also, the methods of torture and the materials used did not match. To the best of our knowledge, neither man was in debt to loan sharks or bookies or had ties to organized crime, so who the fuck killed them and why? It was a total mystery to everyone including me, until one day I found a connection between Hanford and Duplass. A connection I now know I was never meant to see. A connection that cost me my career with the NYPD, and one I now knew was the lynchpin in solving this case.

That connection was the honorable Judge James Faulkner.

Months after the Hanford and Duplass cases had cooled to the point of freezing, I found an old, personal email address of George Hanford. One he hadn't used in several years, which is why the forensic team had missed it early on. From this old account, Hanford had a brief exchange with Judge Faulkner thanking him for a wonderful weekend and for saving his life. Faulkner replied, telling Hanford that it was his pleasure to help and that he was glad for Henry to have made the introduction. The email made hints at the fact that the judge had helped Henry in a similar way a while back. As far as I was concerned, this was a smoking gun. Hard evidence that George Hanford and Henry Duplass knew each other after all. Not only that, but that a powerful New York judge made up this unlikely threesome.

It was right after this discovery that I was thrown off the case and ultimately shit canned. At the time I had no idea why, but the evidence I've found since leaving New York has certainly shed some light on a thing or two. After finding the emails between

Hanford and Judge Faulkner, I searched for any electronic correspondence between the judge and Duplass but came up empty, but what I did find was shocking.

Four years ago, Judge Faulkner wrote a strongly worded and passionate character reference on behalf of Henry Duplass to the Board of Directors of FarmTown Foods, Inc. Apparently, the board had been ready to appoint Duplass to the position months ago but had second thoughts when word got out that he was in the habit of paying for sex with very young women. And even girls, possibly as young as ten-years-old. The Board was all but ready to appoint a different candidate to the position and nuke Duplass until the judge intervened. I have no idea why he did, or how he came to know Duplass, but the judge not only saved his career but made the rumors go away as well. With one letter of recommendation, Duplass was saved from public humiliation and placed right back on top.

This got me thinking about George Hanford and his comment about the Judge 'saving his life,' so I continued to dig until I came across sealed court records regarding a sexual misconduct civil case between George Hanford and Christina Voormann, an eighteen-year-old exotic dancer and sex worker. I paid a tidy sum to have the records unsealed and delivered to my private server, and found that once again, Judge Faulkner had personally intervened in this case. Christina Voormann wasn't eighteen, she was fifteen, and George knew it, so Christina was paid off, and the judge on the case had the records sealed, a clear indication of Judge Faulkner's influence. I don't know why the judge intervened in the lives of these two perverts, but the fact that they both showed up dead not long after couldn't possibly be a coincidence.

Did Faulkner hire a hitman to take Hanford and Duplass out in order to cover his tracks? If so, why torture and mutilate them first? And why bail them out in the first place if you were planning on having them killed in the future? Was the judge a vigilante? Pretending to help these men but secretly planning their demise?

Soon, that question would be answered for me when Judge Faulkner died while on vacation in Miami, Florida. He'd been missing for several days, when his body washed up on the shore near the beach house where he and his wife were staying. He appeared to have drowned, despite the fact that he was a champion collegiate swimmer. Granted, that was a long time ago and the judge appeared to have been drinking heavily the night he died. And while he hadn't been shot and dismembered like the other victims, there was no way in my mind that his death was a coincidence.

Now we had three dead bodies in Florida, New York, New Jersey, not to mention several other unsolved cases from around the country that I was currently investigating possible links to. Businessmen connected to sex crimes who'd either turned up dead or gone missing.

A pattern was emerging and the killer coming into focus. These men all traveled for work, and most were found dead or went missing while away from home. The link between sex trafficked women and out of towners has been well known and documented for a while, but the number of these guys who've ended up dead as Dillinger over the past few years was no series of random acts or coincidences. In fact, the pattern, or lack thereof was so random, it almost suggested meticulous planning.

I sighed, taking a liberal swig of my drink.

Or maybe I'd just been staring at this damn board for too long. Too many nights spent pinning up and staring at photos, receipts, phone records, printed emails, and hundreds of scraps of paper. Month after month, searching for answers to a puzzle I was no longer sure even existed.

The scotch was kicking in and my brain was starting to ache from all the overthinking, so I turned off the lights and stumbled off to bed. I fell asleep just about the second my head hit the pillow, but moments later was jolted awake by a thought.

What if the killer was a traveler, just like his victims?

* * *

Shep

"So?" Marco asked the moment he got into the van. I had a job booked in Franklin, and the kid was such a great sous chef last time, I thought I'd hire him again. Besides, the job would run much smoother with four hands than with only two.

"So, *what*?"

"Come on, man. Don't be like that." He waved

a hand, pressing for more. "The hot author lady."

"What about her?"

"You know. Did you hook up with her or what?"

I frowned. "That's none of your business."

"What are you talking about? Of course it is. I practically set the two of you up. And as your official wingman, I have the right to know every last freaky detail of what went down between the two of you."

"I think I liked you better when you called me 'Chef' and were afraid of me."

Marco folded his arms and shook his head. "This is some serious bro code violations and shit."

"Okay, okay," I conceded. "Evangeline and I went out on a date."

"I knew it, I knew it, I knew it!"

"Cool your jets," I hissed. "It was just one date."

"One date that carried on into the morning," he said gleefully.

"Wrong. Just a date. Dinner, conversation, a little wine. That's it."

"Mm-hmm."

"Are you going to be like this all day?" I grunted.

"Yes, chef," he retorted.

I rolled my eyes and let out a quiet grunt as we pulled into the circular driveway of the mansion where we'd be working today.

"Keep your comments to yourself and your eyes on the food, yeah?"

"Fine," he grumbled, and climbed out of the van.

I grinned, following him.

Clarke

At seven AM sharp there was a knock on my front door.

At least we know the kid can tell time.

"Come on in, the door's open," I yelled from my seat at the evidence board.

"Mornin', Sheriff Clarke," my new deputy said. "I brought coffee, just like you said."

"Not Betty's coffee, right?"

"No, Sheriff. I went across town to the Drillers."

"Thank you, Deputy Jost."

I laughed on the inside anytime a local used the term "across town." Where I'm from, going across town could mean going from Hell's Kitchen to Washington Heights, which could easily take an hour with traffic. In the Holler, cross town travel meant going from the Post Office to the Smiley Freeze Ice Cream Parlor. A trip that took less than seven minutes by car.

"I didn't know they served coffee at the Driller's Club," I said.

"Only between the hours of five to seven. You know, to try an' sober up the really drunk ones."

"They should know that giving coffee to a drunk person doesn't sober them up. It only creates an alert drunk. They'd be better off letting those guys sleep it off."

"Yeah, but they've gotta get 'em outta the bar somehow."

I frowned. "As long as they're not letting anyone in that kind of condition drive."

"No, Sheriff. I think it's safe to say that every patron of the Drillers knows to walk home, halfway in the bag, and completely in the dark."

I raised the Styrofoam cup to my mouth, hopeful that the coffee inside would be better than Betty's. My hope was quickly dashed.

"Jesus Christ, that's fucking horrible," I said, setting the cup down. "What is it with the people in this town? Doesn't anyone know how to brew a good cup of coffee? Human beings have been brewing coffee for centuries, using the crudest of tools. I mean, just by the law of average you'd think someone within the town limits would accidentally pour something drinkable once in a while."

"If you don't mind me asking, sir, if you're so picky about it, why don't you fix your own coffee?"

"Because I don't know how to either. I never had to learn. I'm from New York. There's a good cup of coffee to be found every two blocks."

Deputy Jost pulled out his notepad and pen, made a single pen stroke, then put the pad and pen back in his pocket.

"What was that about?"

"Oh, nothin," he replied.

"Take a seat," I said, motioning to the only chair that didn't have files stacked onto it.

"Thank you, Sheriff."

"Do you know what the most important thing is in the relationship between a sheriff and their deputy?" I asked.

"Trust, Sheriff?"

"No, that's the second most important thing. The *most* important thing is that you do exactly what I say, when I say it, without question or hesitation. If you do so, you may *earn* my trust. Possibly even my respect. Until then I want you to be a robot. A cold, unfeeling, mechanical wonder, designed and programmed to aid and assist me to the best of your ability. Understand?"

"Yes, Sheriff," Jost replied.

"Good. Now, what did you jot down inside your notebook?"

"I made a tally mark," he replied, quickly adding sheepishly, "At the behest of everyone back at the station."

"*Everyone* at the station? You mean Betty and Lt. Fox."

"Yes, sir. Uh, yes Sheriff."

"Why?"

"Apparently, they have a pool on how many times a day you'll bring up the fact that you're from New York City. I was told to mark down a tally when—"

I waved Deputy Jost off. "Alright, alright. I get the picture. Obviously, my office staff has too much free time on their hands. I'll make sure and correct that."

"Oh, I don't wanna get anyone in trouble—"

"Don't worry about it. I have other things I need you to focus on right now. Okay?"

Jost nodded. "Yes, Sheriff."

"Good. Now, that trust I was talking about is a

two-way street, and right now I need you to trust me with something very important. Will you do that, Deputy? Will you trust me?"

"Cross my heart, Sheriff," Jost replied, making the little cross motion over his heart with his index finger.

I smiled and nodded in approval. "Jost, I hired you because I had a feeling that you're a smart and loyal man. Am I right? Was my first impression of you correct?"

"Yes, Sheriff. I mean. I like to think so, sir."

"And humble to boot," I said. "I think the two of us are gonna get on like a house on fire."

The truth was I didn't hire Herman Jost based on any intuition I had about him. I selected him because I knew I'd be able to control him. I needed to kick this investigation into high gear and in order to do that I was going to need help. Help from someone I could easily gaslight and manipulate into doing whatever I needed him to do.

Herman Jost was the youngest of two brothers. The older boy, Craig was killed in Afghanistan and Herman had lived in his brother's shadow all his life. I knew he'd be eager to please and driven by a sense of duty to live up to my expectations of him as his superior officer. The Josts were a poor family, and I was certain Herman would do just about anything to keep his job.

"Deputy Jost, I'm about to read you in on a highly classified case. A case that I've been working since before I arrived here in beautiful Kentucky. A case that my old colleagues in New York have asked me to assist them with.”

I paused before asking, “Does that mention of the NYPD warrant a tally mark in your book, Deputy?”

“No, Sheriff,” Jost replied with a slight grin.

“So, I can trust you? No information about this case leaves this room.”

Jost stood at attention and gave me a crisp salute, “Yes, sir.”

“Alright, at ease. That’s enough of that shit. Lemme tell you what we have so far and what it is I need you to do for me.”

Evangeline

I WAS HARD at work in my room on my laptop outlining my next writing project when Emory called.

"What's up, Mouse?"

"Hey, I just got a call from a sheriff in Kentucky wanting to speak with you."

"Kentucky?" I asked, doing my best to sound calm and unaffected. I'd never stepped foot in Kentucky, let alone done a project there, but any call from law enforcement was never a good thing. "Did he say why he was calling?"

"No, but he asked where he could reach you and I gave him your cell number. I hope that's okay?"

"Of course," I replied.

It's not like I've killed nine people or anything.

Just then my phone buzzed and a number with a 606 area code flashed on the screen.

"I think he's calling me now, so I'm gonna let you go," I said before switching to the incoming call.

"Hello?"

"Good afternoon. Am I speaking with Evangeline Monroe?" a male voice asked.

"Yes, this is her."

"Miss Monroe, my name is Andrew Clarke, I'm a sheriff in Black Sheep Hollow, Kentucky."

"Yes?" I replied as calmly as possible.

"I hope I'm not disturbing you. Your associate, Emory Philips gave me your number."

"That's quite alright. How can I help you, Sheriff?"

"I understand you're currently in Nashville is that correct?"

"Yes, that's right."

"It just so happens that I'm going to be in that area tomorrow. I was wondering if we could meet for a quick conversation."

"What's this all about?"

"I'm working on a case of a sensitive nature, and I believe it would be best to speak in person. Are you staying in town? Is there someplace convenient for us to meet?"

"Sure," I said, doing my best to hide the terror in my voice. "I'm staying at the Westview Hotel and should be here all day tomorrow."

"Wonderful. I'll see you tomorrow and I thank you for your time in advance. I hope you have a wonderful evening."

Sheriff Clarke hung up and I thought I was going to puke. My head swam and my heart thumped inside my chest so hard, I thought I'd break a rib or two. Who the fuck was this guy and what did he want from me?

"Okay, calm down, Evangeline," I said, out loud to myself. "For all you know, he's starting a workshop on sex trafficking in Lexington and wants input on his curriculum. Yeah, that's probably it."

Except, he said he was working on a case.

"He said 'a case of a sensitive nature,' so he's most likely working a sex crime case involving a minor, and he wants your expert opinion on the matter."

Or he's coming here to measure you for a noose fitting.

Shit.

⁕ ⁕ ⁕

Clarke

I was uncharacteristically nervous before my meeting with Evangeline Monroe. In fact, I had to change my undershirt after I sweated through the first one. I couldn't recall ever feeling this way before interviewing a person of interest, but then again, I'd never interviewed someone like her before.

Since starting my investigation into Ms. Evangeline Monroe, I'd managed to learn a great deal about her within a short amount of time. In all fairness, it was my new deputy that put her on my radar in the first place. Working off of the theory that our killer had the ability to travel freely across the country without raising suspicion. Deputy Jost, despite the fact that he had not yet acquired a single hair on his ass yet, proved to be a real hot shot with a laptop. Before I knew it, he was able to map out over a dozen businesses that had employees traveling to the locations of one or all of the murders. Within a week, he'd not only narrowed that list down to a workable number but also generated a short-list of potential suspects. After another week of chasing down dead ends, I was starting to feel like my theory had been nothing more than that.

Five days ago…

"What about her?" Jost asked, pointing to a copy of Health and Wellness magazine featuring a beautiful blonde on the cover.

"She's hot," I replied.

"That's not why I'm showing it to you," he said, opening the magazine and pointing to an article on a woman named Evangeline Monroe. "See? Look. This article lists the dates of her last speaking tour."

"And?"

"And she had engagements booked in several of the cities where victims were found."

"She's also a woman," I stated.

"All due respect, Sheriff, but what's that got to do with the price of corn?"

"Less than eight percent of all known serial killers in the United States are women."

"But not zero percent."

I leaned back in my chair. "You know something, Deputy. You're right. That's not zero. What do we know about her?"

"She's a sexual abuse survivor. Some real bad shit from an early age, too, Sheriff."

"Okay, what else?"

"She works as an advocate for victims of sexual abuse. She co-runs a home for kids called Papillion House, and she writes books about surviving trauma."

"Doesn't sound much like our butcher, does she, Deputy?"

"You said yourself that whoever did this most likely had a personal grudge against the victims or was working for someone who did."

"I did say that."

"So, what if these guys were some of the ones that, you know…"

"Assaulted her as a child?" I finished his sentence.

"Well, yeah."

"Well, that there idea sounds about as thin as a…" I said in my best Kentucky accent, only to stall at an appropriate colloquialism.

"The hide on a mosquito," Jost said, coming to my aid.

I smiled. "Alright. What the hell? let's start a file on her."

* * *

I read her first two books in three days. Those

books, in addition to all my other research on her, painted a remarkable picture of survival and resilience. She'd found a way to elevate herself from victim to activist and I was fascinated to learn how she did it. To learn who the woman behind the pages of those books really was. And most of all, to figure out if she was a killer.

Of course, I went into our meeting with ninety-nine percent certainty that this was going to be a waste of time and must admit that my main motivation for meeting with her was personal. Since the moment I saw her face on that magazine cover, I'd become almost obsessed with her. Not only with her beauty but also the strength she possessed. And so, I was more than happy to follow up on Jost's paper thin theory if it meant meeting Evangeline Monroe face to face.

As I approached her table, I noticed Evangeline Monroe quickly close the lid of her laptop.

"Good morning, Miss Monroe. I'm Sheriff Andrew Clarke, we spoke on the phone yesterday."

I presented my badge, which she barely examined.

"That was fast," I murmured.

She shrugged. "I've seen enough badges in my time to know a real one when I see it."

I chuckled. "It's as real as the police union dues I have to pay every month."

Evangeline smiled politely. "Would you like to join me for coffee?" she asked, gesturing towards the empty chair across from her. She was even more beautiful in person than the pictures in that magazine.

"As a matter of fact, I'd love to," I said, taking a seat. "I haven't had a decent cup of coffee since I left New York and whatever you're drinking smells amazing."

The coffee cups weren't the only ones at the table I'd taken notice of. Evangeline Monroe was not only beautiful, but she clearly had an exquisite set of double-Ds underneath her tight sweater.

She lifted the carafe. "May I pour you a cup, Sheriff?"

"Yes, ma'am, but please, call me Clarke. Everyone else does." I gave her the best law enforcement smile I could muster.

I'm not gonna lie. I wanted her to like me. She was the most beautiful creature I'd seen since leaving New York, and maybe even before that and it had been a long time since I'd gotten laid.

"Cream or sugar?" Evangeline asked.

"Black's great. Thanks," I said, taking the cup.

I swear to Christ, the first sip almost made me come in my pants.

"As good as you'd hoped?" Evangeline asked, sweetly.

I smiled. "Even better."

"On the phone you said you were investigating a murder that took place in New York City last year, is that right?"

"Yes, ma'am."

She cocked her head. "But you're a sheriff in Kentucky, correct?"

"That's right. Before relocating to the Bluegrass State, I'd been a homicide detective in New York for a little over four years."

"Big city homicide detective to small town sheriff." She raised an eyebrow. "Sounds like quite a change."

"Yes, it was, ma'am."

"Okay, if I can call you Clarke you have to all me Evangeline."

"Fair enough," I smiled. "As I was saying about moving to Kentucky. My mother became quite ill several years ago and wanted to live out her remaining days back in the small town she'd grown up in. So, I resigned from the NYPD, sold my brownstone, and took a job as sheriff of Black Sheep Hollow so I could help take care of her."

"You must love your mother very much."

"She's a remarkable woman," I lied.

My nag of a mother still lived in the same shitty Brooklyn apartment I'd been raised in, which was only three blocks away from where she was born and raised. To this day, I think she'd only gone into Manhattan four or five times, tops. After my father died, she'd barely left the block. Thank god for my sisters. Otherwise, I'd have had to stay in New York to help take care of her. And after being blacklisted from the department, would have had to take work as a security guard or a fucking garbage man. I sent a check every month, and my sisters took care of the 'hands on' work. But Evangeline didn't need to know any of that.

"Before moving my dear, sweet mother back

home, I'd been the lead detective on a murder investigation in Manhattan. It broke my heart to have to leave in the middle of working a case, and to be honest, it was tough on my captain and the department as well. So even though I no longer technically work for the NYPD, my old captain will call me from time to time to consult or help them run down leads regarding that case, which still remains open."

She settled her hand over her ample chest. "And one of those leads has brought you to *me*?"

"Yes, but please don't worry. You're not a suspect or under investigation of any kind."

"Phew," she said, mocking wiping sweat from her brow. "So, what is it that I can help you with?"

"My investigation has led me to believe that I may be looking for a man with a job that's transitory in nature. A truck driver, carnival worker, a stagehand of a touring show, that sort of thing."

Evangeline smiled. "I can't remember the last time I was at a carnival, so I'm not sure how I can help you."

"I'm sure it's nothing, but the nights of the murders—"

"There was more than one murder?" Evangeline interrupted.

"Yes, ma'am. One in New York, another in New Jersey, and now possibly a third in another state."

Evangeline furrowed her brow. "How awful."

"It's not a pretty case, that's for sure."

"Sheriff, doesn't the FBI normally investigate cases like these?"

"The body of the first victim was found in New York. My captain wants first dibs on this sick son-ofabitch before the Feds. Besides, the Bureau won't get involved until a pattern has been established between the killings. And no one is quick to cry 'serial killer' these days. The general public have enough to panic about as it is."

"That certainly sounds serious," she breathed out.

"Yes, well after researching all the concerts, sporting events, conferences, etcetera that took place in the tri-state area on or around the time of the murders, I was only able to find a dozen potential matches, which I've narrowed down to three. If my theory is correct, the suspect I'm looking for could very well be working and traveling with the Tortoise Audio/Visual Company out of Houston, the Harlem Globetrotters, or your organization."

Evangeline's eyes widened. "That's quite a trio. I can't say I ever thought I'd be on any kind of list that included Harlem Globetrotters, that's for sure."

"They played games on the nights and locations of all three murders. I shouldn't be telling you all of this, but I want to shoot straight with you. If there is a killer within the ranks of your organization, you could be in serious danger. I've all but ruled out anyone at Tortoise, and so far, I've come up with nothing from the Globetrotters either."

"Have you interviewed the players on the Washington Generals? If anyone is fueled with psychotic rage it would be one of those guys, right? I mean, losing night after night, season after season like that would have to drive you crazy after a while, right?"

"I appreciate your knowledge of novelty basketball, but I'm afraid this is a serious matter. I'm becoming increasingly convinced that my suspect very well may be in your camp."

"I'm sorry, I tend to combat utter fear with humor," she replied.

"I don't want you to be afraid, but I do want you to be alert and attentive to everyone around you. Speaking of that, have you noticed anything strange about anyone working on your tour crew? A bus driver or lighting rigger. Anyone who's triggered any kind of red flag from you?"

"If they had, let me assure you, I would have had them replaced immediately. In fact, every member of my touring staff has undergone thorough background checks. I'm afraid, but happy to say, that an investigation of any of my people is highly unlikely to bear any kind of fruit. Of course, there's always the local union crew guys that help us with every event."

"No, I'm looking for someone who travels along scheduled routes. I'm sure of it."

"May I ask why?"

"That depends," I replied.

"On what?"

"May I ask you to dinner?"

In all my years in law enforcement, I've never once hit on a witness or suspect. Not one time. But something about this woman blew a fuse in my fucking brain and the words rolled out of my mouth before I could stop them.

"I'm not so sure that's a good idea—"

"Before you say no, let me assure you. My request is *mostly* business related. I'd really like to speak with you further about this case, but since I'm working 'off the books' with the NYPD, I have to be careful about where I'm seen and by whom. Given your background, I believe you may be able to bring some much-needed insight into the case."

Evangeline crossed her arms and leaned back in her chair. "Why is that?"

"Because I believe these murders are personal and I don't think the killer is done."

"I still don't see what any of that has to do with me."

"Probably nothing. I'll be straight with you, I'm working on nothing but conjecture and gut instincts right now, and I'm probably wrong. However, if this guy is traveling with your crew, you're my best bet at identifying him before he kills again. Plus, you've been around cold-blooded killers. I read your book. After the horrible things you went though, I'm sure you can spot evil from a mile away."

"You said the dinner invitation was mostly related to the case. What's the rest of it?"

"You. You're the most beautiful, charming, and sophisticated woman I've met in a very long time. Maybe ever. And I believe we'd enjoy each other's company if given the chance."

"That chance being dinner?"

"Tonight, at seven o' clock? I can pick you up here at the hotel or we can meet someplace if you'd like. Do you like Mediterranean food?”

“Honestly, I’m not sure.”

“I know the best place for Kurdish Turkish cuisine. You’ll love it. I can tell you more about the case and you can tell me more about yourself. What do you say?”

* * *

Evangeline

“I’d say that’s an oddly specific choice of food,” I replied.

I only had one more day in Nashville and was planning on catching up on a few emails in the little coffee shop in the hotel lobby tonight. I hadn’t expected a police officer to show up and interrupt my plans, but apparently, today wasn’t going to be a good day.

“My grandparents on my father’s side were Kurds. They were Christian converts, so a lot of my childhood Christmases were spent at Baba and Nana’s house. My favorite memory of those holidays was the food. You’re going to love it.”

Alarm bells were ringing so loudly in my head I feared the sheriff could hear them. How the fuck did the sheriff of Beaver Dick Falls connect the murders of George Hanford and Henry Duplass? And who the hell was the third victim he mentioned? Was it the judge?

Killing the dishonorable Judge James Harron Faulkner was not as satisfactory as I would have liked it to have been. I was working within a tight timeframe, and I also had to make his death look like an accident. While that greatly simplified the job, it meant I didn't get to savor the kill quite as much. It also meant I didn't get to display my victim precisely the way I wanted to, which was very important to me.

"Text me the name of the restaurant and I'll meet you there at seven sharp," I conceded. "I have an early flight home tomorrow morning so I can't make it a late night."

"Dinner and your company are all I ask for." Clarke smiled wide. "And maybe dessert."

This guy was slick. I mean, I could tell that at least half of the things that came out of his mouth were bullshit, but I'm sure his charm, good looks, and expert lying skills worked on most people. Of course, I was a damn sight far from most people and I needed to know if this sheriff had already figured that out yet.

"I'll see you there at seven," Sheriff Clarke said before exiting the café.

As soon as he was out of sight, I opened my laptop and resumed my search into ex-NYPD Homicide Detective/Sheriff Andrew Clarke. A search which revealed all sorts of useful information. The kind of information that let me know that most, if not all, of what he'd told me this morning was utter bullshit. I knew his mother was alive and living in Brooklyn. I also knew he'd been fired from the NYPD for insubordination and unauthorized surveillance on a citizen. There was no way in hell anyone within the New York Police Department would ask Andrew Clarke for the time of day, let alone to assist with an active murder investigation. This guy either thinks he's smarter than everyone, including me, or this little chat of ours was all about sizing me up. Clearly, he didn't learn everything he needed, or he wouldn't have asked me out, other than the obvious reason of wanting to fuck me. Another thing I'm sure he felt he hid well but did not.

I was going to have to play tonight's dinner very carefully. This cop was playing some sort of game and I needed to find out why and exactly how much he knew about me. I'd never killed anyone who wasn't a monster or a predator, let alone someone in law enforcement. But if it came down to my survival or Andrew Clarke's life, Black Sheep Hollow would need to find themselves a new sheriff.

Evangeline

I ARRIVED AT the Taste of Mesopotamia restaurant to find Clarke seated and waiting for me. He'd also ordered for us, as the table was filled with huge plates full of all sorts of delicious looking food.

"Thank you for joining me this evening." Clarke stood as I approached. "You look absolutely beautiful."

Jet black hair and a razor-sharp jawline that would make a Calvin Klein model envious, he wore a dark blue, tailor fit suit without a tie, and he looked fresh off the cover of GQ.

"Such manners from a fellow Yankee," I said, as

Clarke pulled out my chair and made sure I was seated before taking his own again.

"I guess this southern charm is starting to rub off on me. I hope it's okay that I ordered for the table. You said that you didn't have much experience with Kurdish Turkish cuisine, so I ordered a little of everything for us to try."

I waved my hand toward the food. "This is a little?"

Clarke chuckled. "Don't worry. Whatever we don't eat here tonight, will make great leftovers for days. Some of these dishes only get better with time."

Clarke ordered from the wine list, and we fell easily into small talk as we sampled the myriad of appetizers laid out before us. Conversation was easy between us, but my mind was busy trying my best to size him up, and I'm sure he was doing the same with me.

"Why did you decide to become a cop?" I asked after we'd finished our first glass of wine.

"Ah, that old chestnut," Clarke replied.

"I'm sorry. Is that too personal?"

"No, not at all. I guess, like most kids, you end up doing what you do for a living because of your father."

"Your dad was a cop?"

"No, he was a degenerate gambler, a drunk, and a petty criminal."

"Ah, so your door swung the other way," I deduced.

Clarke refilled our glasses before raising his for a toast. I raised mine and he said, "To those who've risen above what this world has to offer. May we continue to climb out of the darkness and into the light.”

We clinked glasses and a lump formed in my throat. “I had no idea you were so poetic.”

“How do you like the food so far?” Clarke asked.

“Oh, my god. Are you joking? I can’t stop eating. Everything is wonderful.”

“I thought you’d like it. I tend to read people pretty well. An occupationally developed skill, I guess.”

“Makes perfect sense. I mean, in your line of work you must spend much of your time talking to people and while doing so you’re likely trying to judge whether they are lying to you or being truthful.”

“See? That’s what I mean. You understand completely. This is why I asked you to come here tonight. I had a feeling you and I would understand one another.”

As much as I hated to admit it, Clarke wasn’t wrong. There was a palpable connection between us that was impossible to ignore. I mean, he was at least half full of shit, and he was a cop, so it’s not like I could trust him in any way or drop my guard for even an instant, but there was something about Andrew Clarke, besides his good looks, that made him very attractive to me.

* * *

Clarke

“How do you stay sane living in a place like Old Sheep Junction?” Evangeline asked as I refilled her glass again.

I burst out laughing, almost spilling as I poured. "Black Sheep Hollow," I corrected.

She raised an eyebrow. "Is that really any better?"

"Better n' what the local kids call it, I'll tell you what," I replied in a mock Kentucky accent.

Evangeline chuckled. "Do you think you'll ever move back to New York?"

"Maybe someday," I replied.

"Someday when it's time to settle down and start a family," she said, pointing to my naked ring finger.

"What can I say? I'm a cliché cop who's married to the job. But look at you. You write books, you're a public speaker, you run a home for abused kids. I can't imagine you have much time for yourself."

Evangeline exhaled. "Not much, but when I do, I try and make it count. However, you're right. I'm definitely a work-a-holic."

"I hope I didn't offend you by saying that."

"I've got a pretty thick skin," she replied.

"I sort of gathered that from your book."

"You read one of my books?"

"Two of them, actually."

"Really?"

"Don't be so surprised. You're a wonderful writer."

"Thank you very much, that's sweet of you to say. I'm just a little shocked. You don't quite fit in with my usual reader demographic. That's all."

"Oh, I don't huh?" I challenged. "What reader demographic do I fit into?"

Evangeline grinned wide. "I'm thinking you're probably a big fan of D.W. Foxblood."

"You think I read romance books?"

"No, not really," she laughed. "If I had to guess, I would say the last thing you read was probably a police blotter or the manual to a handgun."

I winced. "It's kind of painful how accurate that was. Am I that transparent?"

"Actually, no. I think you hold your cards very close to your chest," she replied.

Right now, all I wanted was to be close to *her* chest. I had to have her. It was as simple as that. So far, my gut was telling me there was no way Evangeline was our suspect, and I was looking forward to ruling her out completely. As soon as that happened, I'd make my move.

"I've never been much of a poker player," I said.

"That surprises me. I would have thought as a cop, you'd be an excellent bluffer." She smiled. "No offense."

"None taken. In fact, I think maybe that's why I was never invited to any poker games. Or maybe it's just because I'm an asshole."

It could have been my imagination, but I'd swear Evangeline had some sort of physical reaction when I said that. She shifted in her seat, ever-so-slightly, and her cheeks became flush.

"So, who's the sheriff of Black Sheep Holler while you're away?"

"That would be my new deputy. However, this is the first time I've left town since I took the job, and I'm just hoping my staff doesn't burn the place to the ground while I'm gone."

She cocked her head. "What about your investigation? Are you any closer to finding the guy who killed those men?"

I sighed. "Sometimes a case will reach a point where you feel you're either on the verge of a breakthrough or you're a thousand miles off course, and you can't tell which is true."

She bit her lip. "So, what do you do when that happens?"

"You keep moving forward until the evidence tells you what you need to know."

This was a perfect opportunity for me to casually gather information from Evangeline in order to officially rule her out as a suspect. She knew the first two murders happened in New York and New Jersey, but I'd been careful not to mention the location of the potential third.

"It reminds me of something my uncle used to say. He lived down in Sarasota, and he'd take me sailing during the summer break when I was a kid. He'd say 'Below fifty degrees south, there is no law. Below sixty degrees south, there is no God.'"

Evangeline laughed. "Meaning?"

"I think he meant life is tough no matter which direction you travel, but at some point, you have to choose a direction and set sail."

"Sounds right to me."

"I used to love those summers in Florida. Have you ever been?"

I studied her closely.

"Not yet. Hopefully I'll get an invitation to

speak there sometime. I hear it's beautiful," she replied without a hint of deception.

"Is travel always work related or do ever hit the road for fun?"

She chuckled. "Fun? No. I'm not sure I've done anything 'just for fun' in a hot minute."

"So, it's all work and no play for Evangeline Monroe?"

"I'm afraid the books are far more exciting than the author," she replied.

I looked her straight in the eyes. "Nothing could be further from the truth."

For the next hour we talked easily and openly on a variety of topics, and as the evening went on, I found clever ways to gather information about her, and in doing so, two things became clear to me. I'd all but ruled her out as a suspect and that my desire for her was reaching a boiling point.

* * *

Evangeline

What the hell was this guy's game? For every truth he gave me, he'd follow it up with two lies. Then there were all the little tests. "So, Evangeline. Have you ever been to *Florida*? You know, the state where Judge James L. Faulkner was found dead?" Christ, Clarke thought he was slick and I'm sure this shit worked on the local yokels back in Kentucky, but I saw through him like Casper the friendly cop. My best bet was to play along, lie my ass off, and use his own permanent boner as a weapon against him.

"Look," I said, after our leftovers were brought to the table. "I've had a really nice time tonight, and I'm not sure if this is really appropriate, but would you like to come back to my hotel room for an after-dinner drink?"

"I'm not officially on the clock, so yes, I'd love to," Clarke replied, doing his best to hide the eagerness in his voice.

I smiled. I had Sheriff Clarke right where I needed him.

My phone pealed just as he accepted my 'invitation.'

"Oh, this is Emory, do you mind if I take it?" I asked.

"Not at all," Clarke said.

"Hi, Em."

"Hey, it's the call you requested," Mouse said.

"Oh, no!" I exclaimed with a frown.

"Oh, shit, you're on a date and he's a creeper," she whispered.

"And you have no idea why?" I asked.

"No, we have no idea why… shit, I'm not good at this," Emory said.

"No, the timing's definitely not ideal." I glanced at Clarke. "But I understand. Yes, I can be at my computer in fifteen minutes."

"You must teach me your ways, Obi Wan," Emory hissed, and I nearly bust out laughing.

"No, it's fine. I'll be there as soon as I can." I nodded. "Okay. Bye."

I hung up with a grimace and looked at Clarke.

"I'm so sorry, but an emergency has come up at Papillon House and I have to take care of it. Rain check on the nightcap?"

"Oh, ah, of course."

I stood and he did the same as I gathered my purse. "Gosh, I'm so sorry. I was looking forward to it."

"I could always meet you after," he said.

I forced a smile. "No, it's okay. I honestly don't know how long this will take. Sometimes things like this go into the wee hours of the morning and can be brutal."

"Right."

"The children come first, always," I said, leaning in to kiss his cheek.

It was quick, but it was effective.

"Do you want to take any of this food?" he asked.

"Oh, no, I couldn't," I said. "You take it."

I got the hell out of Dodge before he could follow and rushed back to the hotel. I had to keep him on the hook, but I also had to keep him at arms' length. Keep your enemies closer as they say.

Ten

Evangeline

THE WEATHER FINALLY cleared up two days later, so despite feeling the highly unfamiliar emotion of disappointment, I left Nashville behind and headed to Savannah.

I'd texted with Shep a few times before leaving, and I think the reason I was feeling disappointment over leaving Nashville was because I was going to miss him.

No, that couldn't possibly be it.

"Ms. Monroe?"

I was pulled from my thoughts by the deep voice, and I glanced up at the flight attendant. "Yes?"

"Would you like more wine?"

No, what I want is Shep Waller's face between my legs, but that's not on the menu.

"Yes, wine would be great, thank you."

I paced myself with the wine, since the flight was short, and once we touched down, I headed to my hotel. I didn't have anything on the agenda for the evening, so I took a hot shower, and opened a bottle of wine.

* * *

The next day, my speaking engagement finally wrapped up, and I had just sat down at the table getting ready to sign books when a familiar voice washed over me.

"Will you sign mine first, ma'am?"

I glanced up to find Shep standing in front of me, and I forced myself not to sigh like a love-struck schoolgirl.

"Shepard Waller, what are you doing here?" I demanded, standing and making my way around the table to hug him.

"At the risk of sounding like a stalker, I had a rental property I needed to check on, plus my mama has been buggin' me to visit, so I figured now's a good a time as any."

"And it had nothing to do with the fact you knew I was going to be in town?"

"I'll give you the answer to that question over dinner tonight? What time do you wrap up?"

"Wow, you're pretty pushy for a stalker, I

thought you guys hung back in the bushes." I tapped my lips with my fingertips as though I was in thought. "No, wait, that would make you more like a peeping tom, huh?"

"A bad one, if that's the case. I'm afraid I left my good binoculars at home." Shep smirked. "Would you settle for a hungry Shep? I'll make it worth your while."

"I'd love to join you for dinner," I breathed out. "But I might not get out until late."

"No problem. I'm used to eatin' late. Chef's hours and all."

I grinned. "Right."

"Text me when you're ready and I'll pick you up. Until then, I'll make myself scarce."

I nodded and watched him for a few long seconds as he walked away.

* * *

Shep

I couldn't stop the shit-eatin' grin as I climbed into my rental and headed to my mother's home. To say I was happy that Evangeline accepted my dinner date was an understatement. The truth was, I was fuckin' ecstatic. I hadn't been able to get her out of my head for the last two days, and I knew flying down for the week was a risk, but I wasn't lying when I said I had a rental I needed to check on, or a mother who wanted to see me. Of course, I'd just been here two months ago, but my mother sure as hell wouldn't complain about seeing me again so soon.

I pulled into the driveway and turned off the car, then grabbed my bag and headed to the front door. Ringing the doorbell, I tried the doorknob, unsurprised the door opened, and pushed inside. "Mama?"

"Kitchen!" she called back.

I closed and locked the door, dropping my bag on the floor, then made my way to the back of the house, finding my mother elbows deep in a chicken. I grinned. "What are you doin', woman?" I demanded, wrapping my arms around her from behind and kissing her neck.

"What does it look like I'm doin'?" she sassed. "I'm makin' my boy dinner."

I sighed, crossing my arms and leaning against the counter.

"Well, shit," she breathed out. "You got plans."

"I do."

"It'll keep." She shrugged, giving me her signature, million dollar smile. "You gonna be here tomorrow night?"

I chuckled. "I can be."

"Correct answer, child of my loins." She wrapped the chicken up and set it in the fridge then washed her hands before hugging me. "How was your flight?"

"Good." I hugged her back, then grabbed a beer and sat at the kitchen table. "How are your gutters?"

I'd patched them last time I was in town, but it had been raining heavily over the past month, so wasn't sure how long they'd last. They'd ultimately need to be replaced.

"No leaks," Mom said.

I tipped my beer toward her. "For now."

"For now," she said, pouring a glass of wine and sitting across from me. "Now, tell me about this girl."

I glanced at my wristwatch. "That took you all of four minutes, Mama. A record."

She rolled her eyes. "Tell me everything."

I laughed. "I don't know everything. I just met her."

"Then tell me what you do know."

For the next hour, I filled my mother in on everything I knew about the beautiful Evangeline Monroe. Well, the PG version of it, anyway. Once Mom was satisfied as much as a nosy southern mother could be, I took a quick shower, and finished dressing just as Evangeline texted she'd be ready in about thirty minutes.

I grabbed my keys and told my mother not to wait up before heading out.

* * *

Evangeline

The last reader had lingered a little longer than I would have liked, telling me all about her daughter, mother, and niece who'd all been abused. Of course, not as badly as I had been (her words), but she was convinced her sister's brittle bone disease had been brought on as a result of the sexual trauma she'd experience in high school and wanted to know my thoughts on this phenomenon.

Within my studies, I couldn't recall ever reading any medical journals positing a link between sexual assault and osteogenesis imperfecta, but admittedly, I wasn't a medical doctor, so I did my best to gently guide her to reach out to one. When she said she'd already done that, I was about to recommend her sister talk to a counselor when I was once again interrupted Shep's velvety voice.

"Excuse me, ma'am?"

We turned to face him and the woman, I think her name was Barbara, let out a quiet giggle. "Um, yes?"

"I'm so sorry, I'm Ms. Monroe's publicist, and I have to steal her away for a scheduled interview."

I checked my wrist for a watch that wasn't there. "Oh, is it that time already?"

"Does she really have to go?" Barbara complained. "We were in the middle of such a good conversation."

"I'm afraid so," Shep said. "If she's even a minute late, the people at *Cat Fancy* will chew me out."

"Oh, they're the *worst*," I breathed out. "I keep telling him to take them off the list. But the readership is just so loyal."

"I love Cat Fancy. You don't have to tell me, I'm a subscriber," Barbara said.

Shep took my hand. "Well, then, be sure to look for her article."

I pressed my lips together and forced back a laugh as Shep extracted me from the situation, practically having to put himself between me and the woman before walking me away.

"Oh my god, thank you," I said. "I didn't know how I was going to get out of that."

"I'm not kidding, this bitch with Cat Fancy is scary."

I laughed. "Now Barbara's going to be really upset when she doesn't find an article. I'm going to get a very long letter of annoyance."

"Don't worry about it, they're just doin' their best to 'ride the bull.'"

"Huh?"

"Tryin' to hit that eight-second mark before the buzzer." He settled his hand on my lower back and guided me to the room behind the signing table. "If they can keep you engaged and talking for as long as possible, they will keep doing it, and come back over and over again because you're famous in their eyes, so to them you become their friend and confidante."

"Oh my god, that makes total sense."

He grinned. "You've just gotta figure out how to buck 'em off quicker."

"Or bring you with me to every engagement."

"Or that." Shep chuckled. "Are you good to go, or do you need to pack up?"

"I'm good to go."

"Are you hungry?"

"They actually fed us, so I'm good, unless you need to eat."

He shook his head. "I'm fine. Come on. I'll show you around Savannah."

We walked out to his car, and he drove me down

to Forsythe Park, where he parked, and then he took my hand and we continued along the brick lined streets of the Historic District, walking hand-in-hand, the cool southern evening air chasing away the heat of the day.

I'd never known peace the way I had when I was with Shep. Every man I'd ever known had entered my life as a stranger and left the same way. With Shep, the more I learned about him, and spent time with him, the safer I felt.

"Penny for your thoughts?" Shep asked.

"What? Oh, sorry. Did I go away for a little while?"

"Yeah, but not like I've seen before," he replied.

I stalled. "What do you mean, before?"

"Last week, when you were speaking at the Mandrake House, and a few times since we met, I've got the sense that you sometimes dissociate." He shook his head. "I hope it's okay that I said that. I don't mean to pry or anything—"

"It's okay, Shep. You're not wrong. I'm just surprised you'd notice something like that."

"My mother said I was a sensitive kid, and even though my pops tried to toughen me up, I think that part of me stayed pretty true. It's what made me a good firefighter and now a chef, if you can feel what someone needs before they can even form it into words, your job is half done."

"Oh, yeah? Well, tell me then. What do I want right now?"

"You want two things," Shep replied, confidently. "First, you want one of these."

He leaned down and kissed me gently. Slowly, exquisitely. God, this man knew how to use his mouth, and my body ached with the thought of him using it all over me.

"Okay," I said, once he'd broken the kiss. "You got number one right, what else do I want?"

"You want me to take you to my favorite place in all of Savannah."

"Ooh, sounds fancy."

He cocked his head. "Well, the favorite place of nine-year-old Shepard Waller."

"Hmm." I bit my lip. "That sounds less fancy."

"Come on," he said, guiding me across the street and around the corner to *Professor Norman's House of Magic, Toys, and Games*.

"Your stellar empathic skills told you that I wanted to come to a toy shop?"

"'*The toys and games are merely a ruse for the un-initiated punters,*' Professor Norman himself would say."

I laid my hand on my chest. "Oh, my god. You were a magic kid."

"The words you're looking for are junior prestidigitator."

I scrunched up my face in horror. "Jesus H. Jones, you were a *creepy* magic kid?"

"I was Professor Norman's best and brightest student. I was so gifted at the art, the Professor gave me private lessons for free."

"Is the professor still with us?" I asked.

"Sadly, no. He was already quite old when I was

hanging around here. Somewhere around one hundred and thirty years old as best I could figure," Shep said, holding the shop door open for me.

"A hundred and thirty? Get out of here."

"The professor was a wise and powerful man," Shep said as we entered.

"He was a cranky old bastard who made his living selling gimmicked decks and fake vomit," a middle-aged man said, making his way toward us.

"Evangeline, may I introduce you to the Professor's son?" Shep said, waving his hand toward the man. "Professor Junior."

"Gimmie a break with that shit, will ya?" He gave Shep a gentle slap of the cheek before turning his attention to me. "Evangeline, I'm very pleased to meet you. My name is Lawrence. This is my family's shop."

I smiled. "It's a pleasure to meet you, Lawrence."

"Come on, Larry. Don't tell me you're still the straightest arrow to ever stick in the mud," Shep teased.

Lawrence turned to me with and tsked. "Evangeline. I'm not sure how you met this, this...this... hang about. This *loiterer* but let me tell you something. He's a dreamer and he's never going to amount to anything."

Shep's mouth dropped open in mock disgust. "Did you just call me a *loiterer*?"

"You are the master and chief of loitering."

I did my best to suppress my laughter at the affectionate bickering between these two men.

"You should have seen this little pest back when my father still ran the place," Lawrence said. "He'd hang around for hours and hours without buying a single thing."

"Untrue," Shep said.

"Oh, sure. On occasion you'd scrounge up enough change to buy a false thumb tip or a comic book, but the rest of the time you'd be on that stool next to the counter pestering my father into showing him how to do all the tricks in the shop. And instead of my father doing the smart thing for the business and demanding that you buy the tricks and learn them, he'd always cave in and show you how to do them."

"Pop always did like me best," Shep said with a grin.

"You know, he's not joking." Lawrence wagged his finger. "I half expected the old man to leave you the shop in his will."

"He did, but I thought it would be cruel to keep it from you, so I had the lawyers put it in your name."

"Oh, so I have *you* to thank for all of *this*?"

"You're welcome," Shep replied.

The two men embraced. Complete with the hearty back slapping that always seems to accompany a good ol' fashioned man hug.

"It's good to see you again, Shep. Mom and I still really appreciate everything you did for the family when dad died."

"It's nothing. The least I could do for the professor. You know how much I loved him."

Lawrence shook his head before turning his attention back to me. "This man is as good as they come, Evangeline. Now, I can tell by the look on this kid's face that he's sweet on you, but if you aren't yet convinced about him. Let me tell you, he's a keeper."

"Alright, Larry. Take it down a notch, buddy, or I'll send you some rubber vomit."

I laughed, but I was terrified. I could no longer deny it. I was developing feelings for a man who seemed to be too good to be true, and I couldn't help but be afraid I was going to get hurt, and that none of this would end up going well for either of us.

"Come on, let me show you around," Shep said, taking my hand before walking me up and down the aisles.

As we perused this magical kingdom of toys, Shep kept me entertained with magic tricks and gag props. The aisles were lined with masks, costumes, and magic kits, fake arrows through the head, fake knives, even a fake full-sized guillotine. A house of deception and misdirection. My kind of place indeed.

After a while, we said goodnight to Lawrence and the Norman family magic shop and continued our wonderful stroll through Old Town. Still, as much fun as I was having with Shep, I was unable to step out from under the black cloud hanging above my head. I only hoped Shep couldn't sense my feelings of impending doom. We didn't have much time left together, and I wanted it to be unforgettable. I was enjoying my time with him, and even though I knew it couldn't last, I wanted to at least play pretend for a little while longer.

* * *

Clarke

I returned to Black Sheep Hollow to find my inbox filled with the usual. Noise complaints from warring neighbors. Reports of vandalism and petty theft. Melinda Mayflower, one of our local whores, slipped and fell inside the Nickel and was threatening to sue, but apparently Deputy Jost was able to calm her down after getting Larry to agree to give her seventy-five dollars from the till. The bidding had started at fifty, to which Melinda countered with one hundred. Jost closed the deal at seventy-five, and Ms. Mayflower went along her merry way. Hiring a local boy as my deputy proved to be a wise decision. Jost was far brighter than I'd have thought, and everyone in town seemed to like him. In fact, I had zero fear of leaving him in charge next time I left town, which I hoped would be soon.

Since returning home, I'd been consumed with thoughts of Evangeline. I could barely focus on what little work I had, let alone on the secret case, which I was now sure was heading nowhere. I jerked off to thoughts of her every night. Going so far as to creating AI porn out of pictures I found of her on the internet. I kept thinking about what would have happened that night if she hadn't been called away on an emergency. She wanted me to fuck her, that was clear. I only hoped the invitation

125

inside her pants would still be open the next time we met.

There was no use in trying to concentrate on this petty horseshit anymore. I was about to buzz Betty's desk and tell her that I was leaving early when Jost knocked on my open office door.

"Come on in," I said.

"Hey, Sheriff," Jost said, closing the door behind him before handing me a file folder. "I managed to get Evangeline Monroe's credit card statements from the past six months."

"Find anything interesting?" I asked, perusing the records.

"Nothing out of the ordinary at all. She eats Chinese takeout more than you'd think for someone as fit as she is. She pays her statement, every month, right on time. According to these records, she's about as boring as can be."

There is absolutely nothing boring about Evangeline Monroe.

"Alright, Deputy. Good work. With this and everything else, I suppose we can safely rule out Ms. Monroe as a person of interest."

"Yeah, unless you want to bust her for that unpaid parking ticket," Jost said with a laugh.

"What ticket?" I asked.

"Oh, nothing. She parked her rental car in a no parking zone while in Miami a few months back and got a ticket she still hasn't paid."

My blood ran cold.

"She was in Miami? You're sure?"

"Yup. It's in there, page three I think," he said,

pointing to the file.

Sure enough, Evangeline had rented a car in Miami during the timeframe in which Judge Faulkner 'drowned.' The parking ticket she received was only one block away from the Judge's beach house.

She lied to me.

Holy shit, Evangeline Monroe is the killer.

Evangeline

W E MADE OUR way back to the car and once Shep climbed in, he turned to face me. "Where to, ma'am?"

I bit my lip. "Would you think less of me if I invited you back to my hotel room?"

"There's nothing you could do or say to make me think less of you."

Well, let's not test that theory this soon, bub.

I forced a smile. "Are you sure?"

"I'm sure."

"Just to be clear, I'd like to have sex."

Shep smiled gently as he started the car. "I was moppin' up what you were spillin', beautiful."

"And you're okay with that, knowing what you know about me?" I pressed.

He reached over and took my hand. "Let's put a pin in this until we can focus, hm?"

I nodded and waited rather impatiently until we were at my hotel and safely ensconced in my room. Shep started by kissing me again, and I slid my hands up his chest, dying to see what was hidden under his clothing.

"Talk to me, Lina," he said. "Give me your parameters."

"Parameters?"

"I don't want you doing anything that makes you uncomfortable," Shep said, stroking my cheek.

I bit my lip. "You're the first man who's ever said that to me who I actually believe."

He frowned. "Don't like that, honey."

I sighed. "I don't really like it either, but let me enjoy this moment, okay?"

Shep smiled. "I can do that."

"Can you forget everything you've learned about me so far and fuck me, though? Hard. I like it hard and rough."

"If you promise you'll tell me if something scares you."

"I can do that."

"If you start to fade away, I'll know," he warned.

"I won't."

"Anything I should avoid?"

"Don't say 'good girl,' don't look me in the eyes like this means something, don't call me 'Angel,' and we'll be golden," I said.

"You really want it rough, Lina?"

"I really want it rough, Shep," I confirmed.

His hand went to the base of my throat, and he pushed me up against the wall, before kissing me, his tongue pressing at the seam of my lips.

I opened for him, and my tongue met his as he palmed my breast roughly over my shirt. I arched into his touch, mewling with need, as he continued to play havoc with my nipple.

He moved his mouth to my neck and rasped, "If you don't want your clothes in shreds, take them off and stand at the edge of the bed."

"All of them?" I asked.

"Depends on what you want destroyed."

I shivered and pushed off the wall, starting to remove everything except my panties. The idea of Shep ripping them off excited me to no end.

"Jesus," he hissed as I stepped out of my jeans.

"What's wrong?"

"I knew you'd be beautiful, but… fuck, Lina." His eyes raked over me. "You're perfect."

"Don't be sweet, Shep or this'll never work."

"Right." He crossed his arms and raised an eyebrow. "I don't like to be kept waiting, Evangeline."

I grinned, unbuttoning my blouse. Slowly.

I slid it off, then unhooked my bra and let that fall to the floor. Shep's nostrils flared, and he closed his eyes briefly before looking at me again.

"Bend over the bed and spread your legs," he growled. "Ass high."

It was then he noticed my tattoos.

"You have a thing for butterflies."

"Mmm hmm."

"And this one looks *new*."

"I like to get a new one when I visit a place I like."

"Well, hopefully you're gonna like it here a whole lot more after tonight. Now, get your ass in the air."

I bit the inside of my cheek to keep from letting out an excited squeak as I did exactly as he instructed.

He slid his hand up the inside of one thigh before cupping me over my panties. "Soaked already." His fingers teased the gusset before tugging it down and then the lace was ripped from my body, and I sighed as the cool air hit my already throbbing pussy. He slapped the inside of my right thigh and bit out, "Spread your legs wider, Lina. I'm not gonna tell you again."

I did and was rewarded with his fingers dipping inside of me.

"So, ready," he rasped, leaning down to kiss the small of my back as he wrapped an arm around my waist from behind. "On the bed, on your back. Knees spread."

I didn't hesitate, assuming the position and sliding my heels up so my knees were bent, baring my pussy to him. Shep removed almost all of his clothes.

"I'm going to leave these on," he said, referring to his boxer briefs.

"Why?" I asked with a frown.

"Because I don't want to scare you—"

"You're that big?" I teased.

Jesus, again with the teasing.

He chuckled. "Trust me. We're gonna take this a little slower than you might like, but you'll be happy in the end."

He knelt between my legs, grabbing me behind my knees and lifting my legs higher before burying his face in my pussy. He lapped at me, and I slid my legs over his shoulders grinding against his face as he alternated between assaulting my clit with his tongue and fucking me with it.

I fisted my hands in the comforter and arched into him as I felt an orgasm build but before I could let go, Shep raised his head. I let out a groan of frustration which was interrupted by him dragging my ass to the edge of the mattress where he slid off his boxer briefs, rolled on a condom, sliding the head of his cock through my slick, and finally pressed in half an inch.

"Shep," I begged.

He slid out, then pressed in a little further, then out again.

"You want more?" he asked between his teeth.

"You want a pissed off woman if you don't give it to me now?" I warned.

No hesitation, he buried himself to the hilt.

I let out a cry of ecstasy as his girth filled me and I closed around him, sliding my knees up his sides.

Shep settled his hands on either side of me and started fucking me. Hard… finally. So hard, he grunted with each delicious stroke, and I met his motion with my own, taking him deeper and deeper until I could no longer hold back my orgasm. I hooked one ankle around his back and cried out as my climax hit and then Shep's hand went to my throat, and his hips drove into mine even harder still.

It was deliciously brutal, and I loved every second.

I gasped as he took me over the edge, meeting his eyes for the briefest of seconds. He let out a grunt, closing his as he rocked into me, then his cock pulsed, and I lifted my head, pressing my mouth to his.

His tongue drove into my mouth and a whimper escaped my throat as another orgasm washed over me, but when he slid his hand into my hair and yanked it slightly, I arched my neck and mewed as yet another orgasm built.

My nipples beaded tight as they rubbed against his chest hair, and he hitched my left leg over his hip continuing to rock gently until the gentlest of climaxes rolled over me. Breaking the kiss, he settled me back on the mattress and rolled us onto our sides. "You need more?"

I swallowed, shaking my head as I tried to catch my breath. "If you gave me more, it might kill me."

"That's what I like to hear." He grinned. "Gonna get rid of the condom. Want me to bring you something to clean up with?"

"Yes, that would be nice. Thanks."

He kissed me gently, then headed into the bathroom.

"Are you the kind of guy that likes a fully waxed

pussy?” I asked when he returned.

He cocked his head setting a knee on the bed and pressing a warm washcloth between my legs. “Are you suddenly worried about that now after I just spent the last half-hour worshipping said pussy, Lina?”

I sighed. “My thoughts aren’t always linear.”

He grinned, stretching out beside me again. “I’m the kind of guy that likes whatever you wanna do. Your body, your choice. If I’m asked my personal opinion, I prefer a little somethin’ there, mostly because I like the fact you’re a grown-ass woman, not some pubescent girl, but it might be a little too soon to mention something like that at this juncture.”

“Holy hell, sir, you might just be the perfect man.”

“I have you fooled.” He chuckled, kissing my nose. “Give it some time, you’ll change your mind.”

Just wait until you find out about me.

I forced a smile. “Doubtful.”

“How did you get away?” Shep asked after we’d caught our breath.

“That’s a long story,” I warned.

“I’m not going anywhere,” he said with an encouraging smile. “Unless you’d rather not share. I could, of course read your book.”

“What I’m going to tell you isn’t in the book.”

“Seriously?”

I nodded. “I kept this part out. More specifically, I lied about the details of my escape.”

He cocked his head. “Intriguing.”

“There are some things I needed to keep for me,

you know?"

"Yeah, I get that."

"Tony Sugar had taken me to his house, at least, I think it was his house, and kept me there for about a week before he moved me into an apartment with six other girls. I was confused because the place was so small. And it was filthy. Not at all what he promised. He handed me a coke and told me to drink it and I remember thinking, 'I'm not allowed sweets in the middle of the day,' and being excited because I actually got to have something that was forbidden at home." I pinched the pad between my thumb and index finger. "Silly, right? My mother had already pimped me out to seven men, but my little girl brain went to the fact Coca-Cola was forbidden."

"How old were you?" Shep asked.

"At this point, fourteen."

"We can stop, honey."

"No, I'm okay," I said. "It's important I talk about what happened to me. It means they don't win."

Shep nodded and gave me a squeeze.

"I drank the whole can and soon after started to feel funny. Obviously, I now know I'd been drugged, but back then, I had no idea what had happened and started to panic. Until I passed out. I woke up to find a man I'd never seen before on top of me."

"Jesus," Shep hissed.

"And yet, I couldn't move. My limbs were like jelly. I had no control over them, and I was just stuck." I glanced at Shep. "I will spare you the details of the rest, but this went on for several weeks, until I realized a pattern. Every morning, we were forced to wake up, shower and get ready, which entailed hair and makeup, then we had to take our first dose of 'good girl' pills. I figured out a way to circumvent our captors' and those pills. I'd cheek them, dump the drink down the toilet, stick my finger down my throat, whatever I needed to do to make sure that shit didn't get in my system, then I hid whatever I could. I'd watch the other girls and mimic what they were doing. If they scratched, I'd scratch, if they looked out of it, I did that. And when I was raped, I disassociated."

"I would too."

"Anyway, I had this regular customer who carried a wad of money that he liked to flash whenever we were together. It was disgusting. He'd always peel off an extra hundred dollars and tell me it was just between us, which of course, Tony always found and took. But this got me thinking. And planning. So, the next time this guy requested me, I made sure I was ready. I gathered my stash of pills and followed the girls into the van. I had one chance to do this right."

"Jesus, that must have been scary."

"It was. I was terrified." I took a deep breath. "I arrived in the room, and I offered to pour him a drink, which he accepted. I had already crushed the pills, so I stirred them into his scotch, then handed him the glass. He was naked and stretched out on the bed and he patted the mattress next to him. I said, 'Why don't you drink that while I change into something more comfortable?' He was all for that, so I slipped into the bathroom, leaving the door cracked slightly and watched while he downed his drink." I looked at Shep again. "He was a big guy. Slovenly, so it took a little while for the drugs to kick in. I started to panic a bit, but finally, he was out, and I walked back into the room and grabbed his wallet. He had over three thousand dollars in there, so I took it, along with his credit card. I took a minute to eat some of the snacks in the room because I was starving, then I took his coat, because I didn't have one. I knew I couldn't escape through the front door, but the bathroom window was big enough for me to fit through, so that was really my only option. I locked the hotel door up tight, put a chair under the knob like I'd seen people do in movies, then gathered the rest of the snacks from the room, his coat, the money, and shimmied my way out of the bathroom window. I had no idea where I was, where I was going, but I had three-thousand dollars, food, and a warm coat, so I knew I could survive for a little while."

"You didn't want to go to the police?"

"Let me tell you something about law-enforcement. As soon as they find out you're a prostitute, they either lock you up and lean on you for information about your pimp or johns, or they throw a back seat squad car party for you. Then, once they're done with you, they toss you right back onto the streets where our pimps are waiting to beat the shit out of us for going to the cops in the first place."

"But you were just a kid."

"A lot of times, people that children turn to for help are among the worst perpetrators. How many times have you flipped on the news to hear clergymen, cops, lawyers, and judges have been arrested for abusing children? It happens so often now, the public has become numb. These are exactly the types of men who paid to abuse me over the years," I said.

"Jesus," he hissed.

"You learn very quickly there is little to no one you can trust when you're in this situation. And children have no autonomy over their person as it is, so they are the 'least of these' in every sense of the word. They can't vote, they can't pay taxes, so although, every politician will tell you that children matter, the reality is, they don't. The worst part is that girls are forced to find and recruit other street kids into the business. If we don't, we'd suffer starvation, beatings, or worse."

"That's heartbreaking."

"At first," I agreed. "After a while, you become just as numb as the public."

"Which is why you're trying to change it."

"I'm not sure I *can* change it. The second one trafficker is pulled off the street, two more take their place. It's an epidemic, and there's always a demand that someone is looking to fill. But if I can stop one child from being taken. One child more from being abused. Then I'll feel like I'm doing *something* at least." I sighed. "Maybe."

"What happened after you escaped?"

I ran my finger over his chest distractedly and shrugged. "I met Mouse, um, Emory on the street, uh, she's my VP of intake now and my best friend, really, but we ended up meeting a woman who took us under her wing for a time. She ran a club, an exclusive, high-end club—"

"You joined a sex club?"

"No, we were too young," I said. "She would never let her girls work the club until we came of age and then only if we wanted to. I never did, at least on a professional level. I did like to watch though, which of course, is part of the fun of a club. I'd met a couple of men while I was there and it's where I was really able to figure out if I liked sex, what my limits were, and who I could trust. She taught me that. She also put us through school. College, not grade school." I bit my lip. "I owe her my life."

"You gonna tell me her name?"

"No," I said. "She's a ghost and she likes it that way. But she did take care of me and Mouse, kept us safe, and helped focus our trauma into helping others. She also helped me separate the rape from sex so I could enjoy it. And that's when I figured out I liked to be dominated. I don't want to go so far as to live an entire lifestyle surrounding it, but I do like to play."

"Well, if that changes, you let me know."

"I will, Shep. You don't ever have to worry about me not communicating."

He smiled gently. "You hungry?"

I nodded. "How about we order room service,

then we can do this again?”

I grinned. “Yes, please.”

He grinned and grabbed the phone.

Twelve

Evangeline

"MAY I ASK why you left the fire department?" I asked once our order arrived.

He paused mid-chew, studying me.

I waved my hand. "You don't have to tell me if it's too hard, but I'd really like to know."

He sighed. "It wasn't just one thing."

"Decisions like that rarely are."

"I guess it started with my buddy, Lincoln Marxx. We got the call that there was a bad two-car accident, drunk driver. Linc was on shift with us when we arrived on scene. It was his wife's car, and it was engulfed in flames."

"Holy hell," I breathed out.

Shep nodded. "Lincoln got his little boy, Ezra out, but Jennifer was DOA. She was pregnant with their second baby. Ezra died two days later."

I bit back tears. "Oh my god."

"Yeah, it was a fuckin' nightmare. He quit soon after. But he's with a good woman now. Rides with a club out of Savannah and has a couple of kids."

"Rides with a club?"

"Motorcycle Club. Dogs of Fire. Great bunch of Guys. Goes by Doom and has found his happy. We get together a few times a year."

"It's good you still get together."

"Yeah."

"But you stayed after that?" I pressed.

"Yeah. I stayed on for another three years." He dragged his free hand down his face. "It was a house fire. Four-alarm. Arrived on scene to find a woman standing out front and it took some time to get out of her that her kids were still inside."

"Wait, what? She didn't get them out?"

"It gets worse. She not only didn't get them out, she set the fire. Twelve, eight, and four. The twelve-year-old was able to untie himself—"

"What?" I squeaked.

"The motherfucking cunt had drugged him and tied him to his bed before she set the house on fire," Shep bit out. "What we learned later was whatever she'd put in his drink made it taste funny, so he dumped it down the drain when she wasn't lookin' and was woken up when the fire alarm went off. He got himself loose and went looking for his little sisters. He found the four-year-old, got her out. Hid her from their mama in the bushes around the side of the house but couldn't find the eight-year-old."

"Oh my god, Shep."

"He went back into that goddammed house three times looking for her before we got there and then fought us tooth and nail when we wouldn't let him back in."

"Did you find her?"

"Yeah," he rasped. "Locked in a trunk at the end of the mother's bed."

"Holy hell," I rasped.

"The kid said she'd lock them in there when they were misbehaving," he hissed. "This was one of the wealthiest neighborhoods in all of Savannah. No one had any idea any of this was going on. No one sounded the alarm. No one called CPS, no one had any idea these kids were being abused. She was a single mother with no family, so there was no one looking out for them. She lived on her family's trust fund."

"CPS probably couldn't have helped, Shep. They're working with one hand tied behind their back as it is."

"Probably."

"What happened to the surviving kids?"

"Daegan and Ramsey. They had no surviving relatives, so Doom and Lyric actually took them in."

"Seriously?"

"Yeah. They're really good people."

"Sounds like it."

"And a couple of the fire crew ride with the Dogs, so the kids have both a fire family and a club family that they wouldn't have gotten otherwise."

"That sounds incredible."

"It is."

I stood, making my way to him and cupping his face. "You know you did everything you could, right?"

"Yeah, baby. I don't hold onto that. I just couldn't deal with seeing another dead baby."

"I get that."

"Can I be done baring my soul for today?"

I smiled gently. "For today."

"How about you bare something else?" he suggested, untying my robe.

For the rest of the evening, we forgot the past and just focused on the present, and everything Shep Waller could do with his mouth.

* * *

Shep

Two days later, I drove Evangeline to the airport. She was headed back to Boston, and I was sticking around Savannah for another day or two before flying home to Nashville. I was not happy with this arrangement.

"Will you come to Boston?" she asked, once she'd checked in.

"Yeah."

"Okay, great. Just let me know when you want

to come, and we'll coordinate schedules."

I nodded.

"Hey." She frowned, squeezing my hand. "Where'd you go?"

I sighed. "Not likin' this long distance bullshit, Lina."

"Long distance bullshit?" she challenged. "We'd have to be in a relationship to put that kind of label on it, wouldn't we?"

I slid my hand to her neck and tugged her forward. "Yeah."

I felt her shiver as she met my eyes. "Don't do that, Shep."

"Don't do what?"

"Don't make it harder than it already is. Just let me walk away from you and we can leave it where it is."

"Leave it where it is?" I frowned. "And where is it, Lina?"

"Great sex, good conversation. Friends with—"

"If you say friends with benefits, I'll lose my shit."

"Friends with positive gains?"

I let out a quiet snort. "I swear to Christ, woman, you're not helping."

"Look, I don't do the relationship thing." She patted my chest. "Can we not put a label on it and let it just be great sex for now?"

I sighed, stroking her pulse. "Yeah, we can do that. But I'm going on record that I don't like it."

"Noted."

I leaned down to kiss her. "Text me when you

land."

"I will." She gave me a sassy grin. "Don't fall in love with me, Shep. It won't go well for you."

"Or it could be the best thing for both of us. Don't know unless you try, baby." Her guard suddenly went up again, and I sighed. "Don't do that, Lina."

She met my eyes and then fell against me. "Sorry. I forget sometimes."

"I know." I held her tight for a few precious seconds.

"I need to get through security."

"I'm aware," I growled.

"You're going to have to let me go so I can do that," she pressed.

I gave her a squeeze, then kissed her one more time before letting her walk away. I had a feeling I was gonna regret it, I just didn't know how deep that regret would be.

Evangeline

RETURNING HOME WAS bittersweet. Sweet because I loved my historical home in Salem. It was less than twenty minutes from Papillon House, and it was on the river. But bitter because my heart was starting to feel something for Shep Waller, and I needed to figure out how to shut that down.

The problem was, I didn't really want to shut it down and this thought nearly induced panic. I needed a man like I needed another hole in my head.

"You have reached your destination," the driver's GPS said, pulling me from my thoughts.

The driver pulled the car to the curb, and I slid

out while he grabbed my bag. After thanking him, I wheeled my bag up to my front porch and unlocked my door. Disarming my alarm, I set my bag at the foot of my stairs before locking up again and heading back to my kitchen.

I noticed my cleaner had been there, and there was nothing better than coming home to a clean house, but, admittedly, the absolute best part about returning home was that I got to start a new project file.

After getting water onto boil for tea, I opened my French doors, and stared out at the water for a few blissful minutes, then I fired up my laptop and logged in to my encrypted files database. I didn't keep trophies or incriminating evidence of any kind from my kills. And, if anyone should ever access my computer and snoop around, they'd find absolutely nothing incriminating. However, hidden behind two fire walls, both of which require separate sets of triple identification, is an encoded database of all my projects, past and present. An extensive library on all of my subjects, including their financial history, medical records, travel itineraries, school records. The works. The more I knew about a subject, the more ways I could use that information to trap them and make them suffer.

You can find out what's truly important to a person by looking at their bank statements and calendar. Whatever a person spends their time and money on is what they love the most. You'd be surprised at how many so-called 'family men' would cry harder when I'd threaten to kill their dog than their wife and kids.

The searches for my subjects would often take months. I didn't always know the real names of my victimizers, but my memories of them would often lead me to clues, and clues eventually led me to them. Most of these animals were posing as up-standing citizens, complete with social media pages to help complete their facades. But I'd find them all eventually and when I did, I'd make them pay for their sins.

Of course, there was enough evidence on my laptop and private server to earn me nine life sentences, followed by a ride in the electric chair, but if anyone besides me ever tried (and failed) to access firewall number one, the whole system was set to wipe itself out. I'd even rigged the server with small explosive charges which would detonate inside the case, frying its physical components beyond repair. I could thank Mouse for teaching me the basics of hacking and understanding computers in general. I was fifteen before I even touched a computer keyboard. I didn't even have access to a smartphone as a kid. It was only after I escaped and met Mouse that my tech education started. Mouse was a genius with computers. It's how she survived in the streets. She'd hack ATMs, public utilities, the cable company. We squatted in a vacant apartment for eight months, with full power, heat, and TV service. She'd set us up with the works, and we didn't have to pay a single dime. From the start, Mouse began teaching me everything she knew. In turn, I used my influence over people in person, to get us just about everything else we needed.

My next project was a man named Reginald White and I'd been looking forward to spending some time with him for quite a while. Reggie proved difficult to track down, despite being from, and currently living in, Detroit. For the longest time all I knew about him was his first name. Not even his proper first name at that. I knew he was white, youngish, and a little under six feet tall, but that was about it.

Until three months ago.

The main reason Reggie was hard for me to track was that I had very little idea of what he looked like as he was fond of wearing masks when he violated me. Clowns, demons, ghouls, carved up baby faces, whatever it took to scare the shit out of me, he was into it. He'd play horror movies like Chainsaw Cheerleader Party on his laptop while he would fuck me, and he'd squirt fake blood all over me when he would come. It was disgusting and I loathed every second spent with him. Of course, he'd want me to act scared, which required little work on my part. As well as being a complete pervert, Reggie White legitimately scared me.

Any first-year criminologist will tell you that the behavior of a victimizer will always escalate if it is not stopped. That is to say, if the victimizers themselves are not stopped. I can certainly verify this through my own experience with men like Reginald White. For example, on Reggie's first 'session' with me, that's what Sugar called them, 'sessions with clients.' I suppose it sounded much more professional than 'feeding the prey to the predators.'

The first time I was sent to Reggie he was wearing a store-bought Halloween mask and wielding a cheap rubber butcher knife. Over time, his masks and props would increase in quality and realism, which got me to thinking. Once I'd escaped and left Detroit, Reggie would have simply started over with a different girl. Maybe another of Tony Sugar's or maybe not, but his obsessions were only growing, and he'd have to feed them more over time. His type of obsessive behavior would drive him to increase the quality of his masks. Perhaps even reaching out to and employing custom mask makers.

Knowing this, I set up trace programs on the computers of every mask maker and horror prop maker I could find via a clever virus embedded inside a lucrative potential job offer email. It took me almost three months just to complete that task and only sixty-three percent of the emails were successfully opened. But while I was away on the book tour, I got a hit. *Fantasy Factory Masks and Wigs* in Bridgeport, Connecticut received an order for a 'maggot infested rotting pig's head mask' from an R. White in Detroit, Michigan. His home address was only four blocks away from the hotel where we would meet.

This had to be my subject. And as much as I hated the thought of going back to Detroit, Reggie wasn't the traveling type, so I'd have to hunt him on his own territory. Either way it made no difference really. Reggie and I would have our reunion, but this time I would be the one wearing the mask and *my* knife wouldn't be fake.

Neither would the blood.

* * *

Shep

My phone buzzed as I walked into my mother's house. I saw it was a text from my buddy, Doom, so rather than texting back, I called him.

"Hey, brother," he said.

"Hey. How are Lyric and the kids?"

He chuckled. "Better than I deserve."

"Well, that's not true and you fuckin' know it."

"How about you? You good?"

"I'm actually in town until Tuesday. You got time for a beer?" I asked.

"If you don't come over for dinner while you're here, my head'll be on the block, and you know it. How about tonight? Tell your mom she's welcome."

"Yeah, tonight works. I think Mom's got plans but I'll ask her."

"Perfect. Let's say six unless I text you otherwise."

"Sounds great. See you then."

We rang off and I went to find my mother.

* * *

I pulled up to Doom and Lyric's home just before six, and before I'd even had the chance to get my door open, Daegan and Ramsey were rushing to open it for me.

"Uncle Shep," Ramsey squealed, her tiny hand reaching for mine.

I climbed out of the car and lifted her into my arms, kissing her cheek. "Hey, sweetheart, how's my favorite girl?"

"I got a one-hundred on my spelling test."

"Great job, honey." I set her down and Daegan gave me a fist bump then a side hug. "Hey, bud, you wanna help me with the grocery bags?"

He grinned big. "Sure."

I handed him one of the bags and we headed into the house, with Ramsey chattering away as we walked up the porch steps.

Doom was waiting in the doorway holding their four-year-old, Sterling, looking happier than a pig in slop.

"Look, Daddy, Uncle Shep's here," Ramsey announced. "Uncle Shep's here."

"I see that, baby," Doom said. "Go help your mama, yeah?"

"Okay, Daddy," she said, and skipped off toward the kitchen.

I set the bag I was carrying on the foyer floor and hugged Doom, then we followed Ramsey and Daegan into the kitchen where Lyric was attempting to feed their two-year-old, Aria, who was in a highchair.

Aria appeared to want nothing to do with it and was screaming her head off. Lyric dropped her head back and groaned, then calmly stood and made her way to me, hugging me tightly. "Hello, gorgeous."

"Hi, beautiful."

"Okay, that's quite enough of that," Doom said, setting Sterling on the ground before making his way to their daughter.

Lyric chuckled, releasing me, then wetting a paper towel and cleaning Aria up. "She's overly tired, honey. Do you want to try and get her down?"

"Yeah," Doom said, unbuckling Aria, and lifting her out of the highchair. "Be right back."

Lyric kissed her daughter, then focused on me once Doom left the room. "I can't believe you're here."

I grinned. "I know."

"So, tell me about the woman that brought you here."

"How the hell did you know it was a woman?"

"I didn't until just now."

"Jesus," I hissed. "Why do I keep forgetting you're a lawyer?"

Lyric shrugged with a laugh. "I have no idea."

Ramsey came running into the room, interrupting us. "Mama? Can I have a snack, please?"

Lyric leaned down and stroked her cheek. "Baby, we're going to eat in less than half an hour. Can you wait or is your tummy super rumbly?"

Ramsey rubbed her stomach. "It's kinda rumbly. May I have a banana?"

"You bet, baby." Lyric handed her a banana, and Ramsey skipped off with a 'thank you.'

"They look really happy, sweetheart," I said, sitting at the kitchen island.

"I'm not gonna lie," she said, leaning against the

granite. "It's taken a lot of work to get them to a point where they're not terrified, especially Daegan, but it gets better every day. We do still find him sleeping at the foot of Ramsey's bed on occasion."

I sighed. "Baby steps."

She nodded. "He remembers so much more than she does, and I hate that for him."

"Yeah."

Lyric reached over and squeezed my arm. "I hate it for you, too."

"How's Linc doin'?" I asked.

"He's close to perfect," she said.

"I'm all the way fuckin' perfect," he said, strolling back into the room, and wrapping his arms around his wife, kissing her.

"Other than his bossiness, he is," Lyric agreed, patting his chest. "Get our friend a beer so I can finish dinner and then he can tell us about this woman he flew all the way back home to see."

"I was wonderin' why you were back so soon." Doom raised an eyebrow as he opened the fridge.

"I didn't just come back for a woman," I countered.

Lyric let out a snort as she pulled open the oven, grinning at her husband. "How cute is he?"

Doom grinned handing me a beer before sitting beside me.

Lyric closed the oven door, then leaned over the island. "Tell us *everything*."

I filled them in what I knew about Evangeline, leaving out the R-rated moments, hoping that they'd be satisfied with the little information I provided.

Evangeline

LURING REGGIE WHITE to the location of our reunion was relatively straight forward. From my research, I knew he ordered girls from a service called *Private Encounters* once every month or two. He was not at all particular about the type of girl he was provided with, as long as she was as young as possible. I'd been monitoring Private Encounters' server for weeks, so all I had to do was wait for Reggie to place an order, head his scheduled 'date' off at the pass, and go to his hotel in her place. Reggie used an "anonymous" user account to place the order, but that account was connected to his credit card, making him easy to track. I took care of the actual girl Reggie ordered with a single phone call.

"Hello?"

"Am I speaking with Mia Rose Harris?" I asked, using my best authoritative voice.

"Who is this? How do you know that name?"

"Miss Harris. My name is Special Agent Margaret Denning of the FBI. Please don't hang up, I have some very important information to give you."

"Wh…what kind of information. What do you want?" she asked, already sounding sufficiently panicked.

"I know that you've been working for Private Encounters for the past nine months under the name Ruby, and that you're only sixteen years old."

"You need to talk to m…my l…lawyer."

"Mia, we both know you don't have a lawyer. And even if you did, I'm not with the police. I work for the United States government and under the Patriot Act, have the authority to detain you for violating sex trafficking laws at both the state and federal level. But I don't want to do that."

"Then, what do you want?"

"I'm calling to warn you," I replied.

"Warn me about what?"

"An FBI taskforce will be moving in on Private Encounters early tomorrow morning. We will be seizing not only all business-related equipment, money, weapons, and narcotics found within the various locations owned by Private Encounters, but we will also be arresting all known employees and associates."

"Why are you telling me all this?"

"Because I don't want you to be among those who are arrested. You and the other girls are too young to have your life ruined by these people."

"Why do you care?"

"Because it's my job to care. And believe it or not, I've been exactly where you are."

"If that's true then you know I can't leave. I don't have any money or a car, or anything."

"You have a phone and that's all you need," I replied. "I'm texting you a number right now. As soon as we hang up, I want you to call that number and ask for Emory. She works for an organization called Papillion House, and she'll help you, and as many other girls as you can take along with you. I promise nothing bad will happen to any of you."

"I'm so scared," she said, clearly crying.

"It's okay, sweetheart. Call that number and Emory will send a van and some men who will get you out safe. They'll plan the whole thing out. Okay?"

"Okay," she squeaked.

"Good girl. Okay, I'm going to hang up now. You call Emory as soon as I do, and if you need me, you can call me back on this number. Alright?"

Earlier, Mouse and I had arranged for an extraction team to be assembled here in Detroit and we had two vans standing by. Hopefully Mia would summon the courage to leave and take others with her, but I knew the incredible amount of strength that would take. Of course, there was no FBI task force ready to bust down the doors of Private Encounters, but I needed her to believe there was in order to save her life. I was going to take "Ruby's" place tonight, and once the police found Reggie's body, they'd go looking for her. I couldn't risk her potentially taking the fall for his murder. I wanted her well out of the way and gone for good. Hopefully Mia was more afraid of the FBI than her captors and pimps.

I arrived at the scheduled meeting place for Reggie's date, the illustrious Western Bed Motel by the airport, an hour early. I needed some time to set up, plus I wanted to make sure I'd have time to deal with "Ruby," should she decide against Special Agent Denning's offer and show up after all.

I arrived at the motel in disguise, so as not to be identifiable in any security camera footage. My guess was at least half the cameras were busted anyway as was to be expected in a fleabag motel such as the Western Bed. As soon as I entered the room, I removed the wig, hat, and glasses, donned the boiler suit I'd brought in my bag, along with rubber gloves and booties for over my shoes. My hair was already tied back tight and under a cap. It was critical that I leave no trace of DNA evidence, especially with me working so close to where I'm originally from. There was a secondary reason for my elaborate get up and that was to conceal any and every part of my identity until I was ready to do so. I didn't even want Reggie to know if I was a man or a woman. Of course, the crown jewel of my disguise was my mask. And just like Reggie, I spared no expense when it came to having it crafted just for the occasion.

My plan was to hit Reggie in the neck with a shot of my Nightfall concoction as soon as he walked through the door, giving me just enough time to guide him to the bathroom, where our meeting was to take place. Once I was fully suited and masked up, I hid behind the door, syringe in hand, waiting in the darkness. The roar of nearby planes taking off and landing provided the perfect eerie soundscape, and my heart thumped loudly inside my chest as adrenaline began to course through my veins. I stood in that position for what felt like an eternity until finally I heard the beep of the key card reader, followed by the squeak of the hotel room door opening slowly.

I stayed perfectly still, holding my breath, waiting for him to step into the room and within the range of my needle.

"What the fuck?" he growled, still standing in the doorway. "I said that bitch better already be on the bed when I get here." His voice was muffled, sounding like he was already wearing a mask.

I was afraid he might leave, but after a few tense moments he finally entered the room, letting the door close behind him. As soon as it did, I moved in on him, syringe in hand, but he saw me coming and turned to face me. Having lost the element of surprise I threw my body weight at him, checking him with my shoulder as hard as I could, sending us both onto the bed.

We landed, face to mask, and Reggie quickly

wrapped both arms around me, preventing me from sticking him. Unable to do anything else, I reared back and headbutted him as hard as possible, aiming as best I could for the bridge of his nose. The impact of the hit was so hard, I saw stars and nearly passed out, but Reggie loosened his grip just long enough for me to jab him in the thigh.

Seconds after I pressed the plunder down, Reggie started going night, night, so I quickly got him up to his feet and marched him towards the bathroom. Blood poured from underneath his mask, leaving a crimson trail along the matted motel carpet. For a moment I felt a little sorry for whoever was going to have to clean up this crime scene, but then I figured I was providing job security to those who do that sort of work for a living.

"That's it, left foot, right foot," I said, encouraging Reggie all the way to the bathroom and into the tub.

"Are we taking a bath?" Reggie slurred as he climbed inside.

"I'm going to give you a very special bath, all your own when you wake up."

"When…I…wake…" Reggie's words trailed off and he fell into a deep sleep.

It took me a while to find the right balance of drugs for the perfect 'Nightfall' recipe. I even had to dose myself a couple of time to better understand the drugs' effects. I needed a concoction that would make my subjects highly suggestable and amiable after the early stage of introducing the drug, and then rendered unconscious for a controlled amount of time. Of course, body mass and a few other factors play into how much Nightfall needs to be administered, but it's not like I'm gonna be sued for malpractice if I get the dose a little wrong from time to time.

Now that he was out cold, I got my first good look at Reggie's newest mask, a disturbingly realistic, maggot infested, rotting, pig's head. A truly disgusting work of art. Of course, I couldn't find fault with the mask maker. How could they ever know how this sick maniac intended to use what they'd made for him? Nor could the person who made mine. Of course, I wouldn't know just how well my mask would work until Reggie saw me in it. But first it was time to unmask the man who'd terrorized me for so long.

I took a deep breath and undid the leather straps that secured the mask to his face before sliding it off, finally revealing the face of Reginald White. A wave of terror washing over me as I looked into his unassuming, wholly unremarkable face.

In my research, I've found that an alarmingly large number of women believe wholeheartedly that they would know a sexual predator if they encountered one. That their intuition would sound off some sort of internal alarm bell. That they are excellent judges of who they can trust with their children. If you could take one look at the face of Reggie White, you'd know what I know. Successful predators blend in with society, they don't often stick out. They can be your sweet, quiet, neighbor. Or that nice young man who sits next to you at church. In fact, most serial sex offenders tend to be quite religious. They might even see their abuse as passing God's judgement on his victims. The soft, doughy, plain ol' face of Reginald White would stick out like a sore thumb in many police lineups, but I knew the truth. I knew the true nature of this man, and today a face from his past would pass judgement on him. Then, she would sentence him.

"My… head. My head hurts," Reggie said, starting to regain consciousness.

"Don't worry about that," I said, from behind my mask. I'd gotten into character while Reggie was having his last temporary nap and was sitting on the toilet, facing him.

I'd stripped him bare and bound his hands and feet with cable ties and duct tape, which I then fastened to the shower handle above the molded soap dish.

I never used exotic tools or products of any kind when working on a project. I tried to leave as little trace of myself as possible and only involve other people when absolutely necessary in this case, that meant hiring an artist to make me a custom mask. Although I'd worn plenty of disguises, masks had never been a part of the equation until now. I *wanted* my subjects to know it was me who was hurting them. That I, myself, was sealing their doom.

Tonight, however. That honor would go to someone else.

Reginald began to squirm and wriggle around in the tub. "Wha… What the fuck is going on here?"

"Shhhhh," I whispered, holding a finger to my masked lips.

Reginald focused on me for the first time and his eyes grew wide. "What the fuck is this? Who are you?"

I answered his question with a stun gun to the ribs. Reginald writhed in clench jawed agony.

"Talk again without permission, and it'll be your balls," I warned. "Now, look at me."

Reginald turned his face towards me. Dried blood was caked down his face and chest. His nose, clearly broken, had swollen to twice its normal size. Tears streamed down his face.

"No," he hissed.

"You know exactly who I am," I said. "Say my name."

"That's impossible. She's dead. You're just wearing a—"

I hit him with 30,000 volts directly to his nuts, causing him to convulse and piss himself.

Once I was sure he could think clearly again, I asked again, "Who am I?"

"Jessica," he said through sobs.

I nodded. "That's right, Reggie, it's your sister, Jessica."

"Why are you doing this to me? Why are you dressed like her?"

I moved in to stun him again, and he began to beg.

"Okay, okay, you're Jessica. Please don't hurt me anymore."

"Did I ever beg you to stop?" I asked.

Reggie's eyes widened more.

"Do you remember?" I continued. "Did I ever beg for you to stop when you were raping me?"

"I never…I loved her…I loved you," Reginald blubbered through blood and snot.

Once I'd found his identity, research on Reginal White proved quite productive in the most horrible of ways. Through my sleuthing I found juvenile criminal court records (all officially sealed, of course) of a young Reginald David White. According to police and court records, at the age of twelve Reggie developed an obsessive fascination with his fourteen-year-old sister, Jessica. There were many spying incidents and even two molestation attempts before Reggie's parents enrolled him in a boarding school in upstate New York. However, the night before he was set to go off to school, he attacked and raped his sister. Even though he was two years younger than Jessica, Reggie was already five inches taller and thirty pounds heavier than her and was able to overpower her while she was sleeping.

The next morning, when Jessica didn't show up for breakfast, Mrs. White went to her room to find Jessica naked and wrapped only in a sheet. Blood was smeared between her legs and had clearly been sexually assaulted. She was curled up in the fetal position and completely catatonic.

The Whites immediately called the police and Reggie was taken into custody but refused to admit to anything. He claimed he was asleep in his bed the whole night, trying to, "Get a good night's sleep before being shipped off to the death camp in the morning."

After months of intense psychotherapy, Jessica finally began to talk, and had even began to show interest in returning to high school soon. Until one day Mrs. White came home from work to find Jessica's lifeless body hanging from the chandelier in her room.

Reggie was eventually released due to a lack of evidence. No prints were found on Jessica's body, and no semen was recovered. At the end of the day, the District Attorney simply didn't have enough evidence against Reggie to build a case against him, but I did.

I had the mask made in Jessica's image using photos from the police files and her social media tribute page as references. Tonight, Jessica was going to see justice done, even if it had to be through my eyes.

"You raped me, Reggie," I said.

"I loved you."

"You killed me."

"No, no. That's not true. You killed yourself before you could see the truth."

"The truth? The truth is that you should have gone to prison for what you did to me. You should have been executed for your crimes."

"Part of me died when you did," he cried.

"*All* of me died when you raped me."

"Please forgive me. I swear to God, I never wanted to hurt you. I loved you."

"God didn't stop you from raping me, why should he spare you from your judgement?"

"You have to admit that we had a connection,"

he breathed out. "You were so pretty, and you smelled so good. Mama said I wasn't supposed to touch you, but I couldn't help it."

"You should have listened to Mama," I growled.

"Somebody help me, ple—" was all Reggie got out before I tazed him in the middle of his chest. While subdued, I placed a ball gag in his mouth and secured the straps around his head.

"As much as I was enjoying it, I'm afraid our conversation is over," I said sweetly. "Now, you're going to know what it's like to be a victim. You're going to find out how it feels to be in one of those horror movies you love so much. That's why I put you in the tub."

Reggie continued to wriggle and moan, but that was all he could do. He belonged to the avenging ghost of Jessica White now.

The hours to come would see me do some of my finest work, and I had to give credit where credit was due. Every punishment dolled out that night was based on the horror movies that Reggie had forced me to watch.

Wrapping Reggie's head in barbed wire and rolling over it with a rolling pin was straight out of Killer in the Kitchen. Shaving his nipples off was obviously taken from Clown Camp II. And then, there were the stabbings. I must have stuck that sick sonofabitch with a dozen different implements all over his body. From butcher's knives to corkscrews. If it showed up in a movie, I stuck it somewhere. The tub was almost half full of blood before he started passing out.

"No way. You're not getting off that easy," I said, shoving smelling salts under his shattered nose to revive him just before slicing his right ear off with a straight razor. Of course, his cries of pain were a lot more muffled after cutting his tongue out. I had to remove the ball gag every once in a while, so he wouldn't choke to death on his own blood, but it was worth the effort to recreate that famous scene in an Eye for a Tongue.

And so, it went until we reached the finale of our theater of the grotesque. Reginald White had been sliced and diced on for around two hours straight and was now at the point of bleeding to death. Of course, after all that, I wasn't about to let him die peacefully.

"I saved the best for last, dear brother," I said, reaching into my bag. "I know your favorite movie of all time is Chainsaw Cheerleader Party so what do you say? Shall we get this party started?" I pulled the rip cord on the portable trimming saw and it fired right up.

"I'm sorry it's not a full-sized model, like in the movie, but those are way too bulky and loud," I said.

Reggie hardly had any fight left in him at that point. In fact, he barely moved at all when I took his right arm off.

Evangeline

I EXITED THE market and walked to the parking lot where I found Sheriff Andrew Clarke leaning against my car, waiting for me.

"Wh…what are you doing here? In Boston? Standing in front of my car…and me?"

"Surprise," Clarke said, casually.

My shock began to turn to fear.

"With all the traveling you've been doing lately, I thought I'd better come to you, or we might never see each other again."

"Traveling I've been doing? Have you been following me?"

"Just keeping tabs on a person of interest, that's

all.”

“I thought you said I *wasn’t* a person of interest.”

“Let’s just say since we first met, you’ve become more interesting by the minute.”

Clarke’s demeanor told me he had the upper hand. He obviously knew something I didn’t, but he didn’t have his gun drawn and I wasn’t in cuffs.

“You want to tell me what this is all really about?”

“You wanna tell me how you got that shiner?” he asked.

I brushed my hair over my right eye.

“I’m guessing Reginald White gave you that the night you killed him. He must have put up some fight, am I right?”

Fear turned to terror. “What the hell are you talking about?”

“Don’t do that Evangeline. We both know you’re too smart to play dumb. Get in my car.” He unlocked his car and held the passenger door open for me.

“What a gentleman,” I said snidely.

“Before you get in, I have to frisk you for any weapons.”

“Go fuck yourself,” I snapped.

“Evangeline. We both know I could arrest you right here and now, but I don’t want to do that. All I want to do is get into the car and talk but before we do that, I need to know that I’m safe.”

“Cop a feel, lose a finger,” I said, slowly raising my hands above my head.

"Okay, all clear," he said after a brief, and non-grabby frisk. "Thank you."

Once inside the car, Clarke started, "I know you were in Detroit the night Reginald White was killed and I know it was you who killed him."

"Reginald who?" I asked.

Clarke huffed. "I thought we were gonna talk."

"We're talking. You're accusing me of murder and I'm telling you for the second time now to go fuck yourself."

"Okay, fine. You don't want to play straight with me? Let me do all the talking then. I know you killed Reginald White, and I can prove it. I also suspect you of killing Judge Faulkner, George Hanford, and Henry Duplass, and have enough circumstantial evidence to arrest you for those crimes as well."

"What about JFK's assassination?" I challenged. "Did I kill him too?"

"The only reason that you're in my car instead of a jail cell is because of me. Believe me when I tell you that I am the only friend you have in the whole world right now. One phone call and I can write my own ticket within any law enforcement agency in the country. Catching a female serial killer, are you kidding me? The book deal alone would make me millions. You, on the other hand, would be tried and convicted of multiple homicides and would go straight to death row inside a maximum-security penitentiary."

"If you're so sure I'm guilty, why don't you make your move? Bring me in and play the big hero.”

“Because I don’t care that those men are dead, and I don’t care that you killed them. In fact, I understand why you did it. Even more, I applaud the fact that you’ve killed at least four men and have somehow managed to fly under the radar of both the police and the FBI.”

I studied Clarke’s face intently. I’d heard him spit out enough bullshit to know he was telling me the truth. Although I still had no idea what his game was.

“If your plan is to blackmail me, I suggest you check my financial records closely. Everything I earn goes into Papillion House. And if you try and take one red cent from those children, I won’t need a weapon to stop you.”

“There she is,” Clarke said with a sly smile.

“What are you talking about?”

“The entire time I’ve spent with you I’ve tried to picture you as a killer, and I could never do it. My brain simply couldn’t draw a parallel between the woman I knew and a cold-blooded butcher, but now I see her.”

“What the fuck do you want, Clarke?”

“That’s not the question. The question is what I can do for you, and the answer to that is twofold. First, I can keep you out of prison by staying quiet about your extracurricular activities. Second, I can *help* you continue without getting caught.”

“What?” I asked, truly unsure of what I’d just heard. “You want to *help* me?”

“It’s only a matter of time before someone in law

enforcement finds you. Until now you've been clever in not establishing obvious patterns, and no one besides me has put the pieces together, but if I can find you, someone else can too. They can and they will. If you let me assist you, I can not only help cover your tracks, but teach you how not to leave them in the first place."

"Why would you want to help me?"

"To put it simply, I believe in your cause, and I've lost faith in mine. I've seen a lot of horrible people do truly fucked up things to people who they claim to love. Most of the time, there was little I could do about it. Even with a badge and a gun, my hands are tied. But you have the ability to balance the scales of justice with your own two hands, and I want to help you do that."

"If that's the simple answer, what's the complex one?"

"I want to help and protect you because I'm in love with you, Evangeline."

"We went on one date, Clarke, you can't be in love with me."

"I've been studying you for months. I know you. I understand you. You and I, we're not like other people. We both know full well how cruel and dark the world can be, and we both decided to do something about it. I became a cop, and you became a vigilante. Is there really any difference when it comes to bringing human filth to justice? I mean, when I arrest some pedophile piece of shit, I'm hoping and praying he'll be locked up for life or put to death. But the truth is that fucking scumbag will be

back on the streets within six months and we both
know it. You simply make sure that doesn't happen.
How can I judge you for that when we both wanted
the same outcome?"

"So, you want to help me commit murder because you love me?"

"Is that really so hard to believe? You are the
most beautiful woman I've ever laid eyes on. And
you're clearly the bravest of souls. You're intelli-
gent, funny, and know how to handle yourself. How
could I not fall in love with you?"

"I assume the price for your silence and protec-
tion is sex."

Clarke's face fell. "No, no, you don't understand. I respect you. I want us to be together. I'd
never treat you like that. Like a whore. I'm only
hoping that in time you'll learn to love me the way
I love you. I want to earn your trust and respect. I'd
also hoped that you'd want to have sex with me like
you did the night of our first date."

Clarke looked like a lovesick puppy.

A puppy I may have to put down if I couldn't
find a way to get him out of my henhouse.

"If you know me so well, you know I need time
to process."

"Of course. You have forty-eight hours to let me
know if we're in this together or on opposite sides
of the law."

I nodded and opened the door.

"Be smart, Evangeline," he added as I slid out of
his car.

I walked as calmly as I could to my own and then

headed home, calling Shep on the way.

He answered on the first ring. "Hey, beautiful, to what do I owe the pleasure?"

"Ah, I was wondering if you'd like some company for a few days?"

"Is that company you?" he joked.

"Funny."

"Yeah, you're always welcome. Give me your flight details and I'll pick you up."

"I can grab a car if you're working," I countered.

"Let's start with your flight details and go from there."

"Okay, I'll text them to you when I'm back at my computer."

"You okay?"

"I will be," I said, pulling up to my home and pulling into my garage.

"You sound off, what's goin' on?"

"I'll fill you in when we're face-to-face."

He sighed. "Shit, that doesn't sound good."

"It's fine. I just need to see you."

"Okay, well, then do your thing."

"Thanks, Shep."

"You bet. You sure you're okay?"

"Yes. I'm sure," I lied.

"Okay, honey. See you soon."

"See you soon," I parroted, and then we rang off.

I rushed inside and found a red-eye to Nashville, then fired off a text with my flight information to Shep. Once he confirmed he could pick me up, I packed a bag, then let the office know I'd be gone for a few days. Luckily, they were used to me disappearing for days at a time, so they were prepared.

* * *

Shep ended up having an early job, so I grabbed a car and headed to the same hotel I'd stayed at previously. It gave me some time to decompress after the flight and I was even able to grab a nap, although, it was a fitful one.

Shep picked me up just before six and his lips were on mine the second I opened the door.

"Hey, beautiful."

"Well, hi, yourself," I breathed out.

"Jesus, I missed you."

I smiled. "What did I say about not falling in love with me."

He laughed. "You're not the boss of me."

"Hm-mm," I sassed. "So you say."

"If we didn't have a reservation and Charlie wasn't a good friend, I'd blow dinner off and fuck you right now."

I shivered. "How close of a friend?"

"Close enough to keep my commitment."

I wrinkled my nose. "Then stop tempting me and let's go."

He frowned and I cocked my head. "What?"

"What the fuck happened to your eye?"

"Oh, crap, I thought I covered that enough." I let out a sigh, rushing to the mirror. "I was unloading my dishwasher and smacked it when I opened a cabinet."

"Let me look at it," he demanded.

"It's fine, Shep. Seriously. Just a little bruise. Nothing's broken. I had it all checked out," I lied. "Just ice and ibuprofen, and it'll be gone in a few days."

"Does it still hurt?"

"Not much."

"Let me know if that changes."

"I will," I promised.

He kissed me once more and led me down to his truck.

Once at the restaurant, we were seated near the window overlooking a gorgeous park, and the chef came out to greet us within minutes. He and Shep hugged, then Shep introduced us.

"Charlie gave me my very first job as a chef. Well, first as a part-time sous chef, part-time dishwasher, but eventually—"

"Eventually, he became useful in the kitchen. And then, as soon as he knew his elbow from a frying pan, was off on his own, cooking for fancy people. And now, he brings a fancy woman into my restaurant."

"It's true. I owe all my success to Charlie."

"That's all I wanted to hear. Now, I can go into the kitchen and put the finishing touches on your first course."

"He's the best, isn't he?" Shep asked.

"You're the best," I said, taking his hand in mine. "Everywhere we go, you're like a beacon of light or something."

"Are you calling me a lighthouse?"

I laughed. "I guess I am."

Just then Charlie returned with our soups.

"Our soup du jour is a beautiful gazpacho made from vegetables grown in our very own garden. Please enjoy."

I blew on my spoon before taking a sip of the beautifully presented soup but found it to be far from scalding hot.

"What's the matter? Is your gazpacho okay?" Shep asked.

"I don't want to embarrass your friend by sending this back, but they forgot to heat mine up. It's completely cold."

Shep smiled, stifling a laugh. "Gazpacho is typically served chilled. Would you like them to bring you something else?"

I hid my face in my hands. "Don't you dare," I said, feeling completely mortified. "I'm going to eat every spoonful of this and you're not going to say a single word. Understand?"

"Of course," Shep said, nodding in agreement, just before waving Charlie over.

"How is your gazpacho?" Charlie asked.

"Well, Evangeline told me it's the best gazpacho she's had in her entire life, but to tell you the truth, I've never been a cold soup kind of guy."

"Say no more, I'll bring you both a selection of appetizers. It'll be my pleasure."

"Thank you, Chuck," Shep said.

"Boy, you are quite the charmer, aren't you?"

But Shep's expression suddenly turned serious.

"You, okay?" I asked.

"Have you ever had trouble with stalkers? Being a famous author and all that?"

I laughed. "If I were famous we'd have gotten a better table tonight."

"Don't look now, but there's a guy standing outside, and he's staring right at us through the window. When I say I want you to casually glance to your left, but do not react to his presence in any way. Got it?"

I smiled and nodded.

"Good," Shep replied, followed by a fake laugh, and then, "Okay, now."

I slowly and calmly looked out the window to our left to see Clarke standing on the sidewalk, staring directly at us. The instant we made eye contact, he smiled and waved.

My heart jumped into my throat.

"Do you know that guy?" Shep asked.

I somehow found the strength to paste on a smile through my terror and wave back.

"Actually, I do. Will you please excuse me for a minute? I should go talk to him," I said, practically sprinting for the exit."

Clarke was waiting to greet me with open arms.

"What the hell are you doing here?" I asked, my phony smile still in place.

As we hugged Clarke growled into my ear, "Who the fuck is this guy you're with?"

I broke our embrace and looked through the window to find Shep watching us intently.

"Shep is a friend who I met last time I was in Nashville. He catered an event where I was the speaker. He's a chef and he invited me here to his friend's restaurant."

"Ah, that explains everything except what the fuck you're doing in Nashville, when you're supposed to be giving me an answer."

"I'm confused. You said I had forty-eight hours to let you know. I left town to clear my head and think—"

"Don't try and fuck with me, Evangeline. I gave you that time to think about my offer as a courtesy to you. The decision has already been made, hasn't it? I mean, what other choice do you have?"

"Choice about what?" I heard Shep's voice ring out from behind me.

"I'm sorry?" Clarke asked.

"Pardon me for interrupting, but Evangeline left our table so quickly, I just wanted to make sure everything was okay."

"I'm alright, thank you, Shep. This is Andrew Clarke. He's an old acquaintance."

Clarke squeezed out the word "friend" just as I was saying acquaintance.

"Yes, Clarke is an old friendly acquaintance."

"Pleased to meet you, Andrew," Shep said, extending his hand.

"Nice to meet you, Shep. Please, call me Clarke."

"Clarke saw us in the window and stopped to say hi," I said.

"Yeah, it was kinda funny running into Evangeline here in Nashville rather than where she's supposed to be."

"*Supposed* to be?" Shep asked.

"Ah, you know what I mean. Where I'd normally find her."

"I see," Shep said, sounding unconvinced.

"How do you know Evangeline?" Clarke asked.

"We met just a little while ago and found out quickly that we enjoy each other's company quite a bit," I said.

Clark broke into an unsettling smile. "Is that so? Two little lovebirds in the making. Isn't that adorable."

"Yeah, well. We should probably get back inside before our cold soup gets warm," Shep said before turning to me. "You okay to come back with me or does your friend Clarke need you to make some sort of choice? I heard y'all right, didn't I? Clarke wanted you to make a choice about something. Sounded important too."

Clarke shook his head. "Nothing we need to bother you with. Besides, I think she knows what she needs to do about Reggie."

"Goodnight, then," Shep said, taking me by the arm and leading me back into the restaurant.

Shep peeled off three hundred-dollar bills and placed them on the table.

"I'll drive you home," Shep said, his voice tight.

"I can grab a car," I countered.

He leaned down, close to my ear and bit out, "Get your ass out to the parking lot and into my truck, Lina. I'm not gonna say it again."

I took a deep breath and stood, snatching my purse off the table with a huff, then led him out of the restaurant.

Evangeline

ONCE IN HIS truck, we drove the opposite way of my hotel.

"Where are we going, Shep?"

"My place," he said, his knuckles bleached white as he gripped the steering wheel.

"And why are we going to your place?"

"Because we're going to talk."

"What if I don't want to talk?"

"Don't give a fuck."

I sighed. "I'm getting that."

"You scared of me, Lina?"

"Of course I'm not afraid of you. What a ridicul—" I cut myself off and scoffed. "Shit. I get it now. If I'd lied and said I was scared, this would all be over, wouldn't it? You'd drop me back at my hotel and I'd be blissfully left alone."

He reached over and took my hand. "We're gonna talk."

"Well, make it quick, Shep," I hissed, tugging my hand away. "I have things to do."

"You came to town to see me, beautiful. What other things did you have to do?"

I huffed. I hated when he was logical and shit. "I came to fuck you, not to converse with you, Shep."

"Multitask, Lina."

We pulled up to a sweet little brick home just outside the city center, and Shep made his way to my side of the car and pulled open the door. I debated whether or not I would push his limits, but ultimately, unbuckled my seatbelt and climbed out.

"Smart choice," he retorted, leading me up the stairs of his porch and unlocking his front door.

Once inside, I didn't have a chance to admire his home, as he locked up again, dropping his keys on the console at the back of his sofa, and then I was shoved against the wall and kissed like he was a dying man, and I was his last breath.

I fisted my hands in his shirt and kissed him back, fighting my base instincts to come to my senses, which I did, far too late. "Wait," I panted out. "I thought we were going to talk."

"Can Clarke do that to you, Lina?" he hissed.

"Wha…what?"

He dragged his hands down his face. "I don't know what game you're playing, baby, but three's a crowd where I come from.”

“You don’t actually think I’m with Clarke?”

“He sure as hell thinks *he’s* with *you*. I heard him tell you to make your choice. I’m not blind or deaf and I’m certainly not stupid.”

“No, you’re not stupid, but you’re wrong about Clarke.”

“I swear I could see into his soul, Lina. You have no idea what kind of man that guy is.”

I scowled. “I know exactly what kind of man Andrew Clarke is.”

“Oh yeah?”

“Yeah.”

“And just how long have you been fucking him?”

I scoffed. “That’s none of your goddammed business.”

He slid his hand between my legs and growled, “It absolutely is my goddammed business, Lina. You are *mine*.”

I hissed in irritation at the reaction my body had to his touch. My pussy immediately flooded, and I leaned into his touch.

“Fuck it,” he snapped, leaning down and throwing me gently over his shoulder.

“Shep!” I squeaked, pounding on his back as he carried me down a hallway. “Put me down.”

He did. Dropped me unceremoniously onto his bed. A large four poster that looked like it had been hand carved. “Shep—”

“Hush,” he hissed. “Do not move.”

He disappeared into his closet, returning holding

rope.

"What the hell are you going to do with that?" I demanded.

"I'm going to bind you," he said.

"What?" I rasped, my body once again flooding with desire.

"How much, Lina?" He raised an eyebrow. "A simple spread eagle or Shibari?"

My eyes widened. "You know Shibari?"

"I know a lotta things," he said, leaning over me and gripping my chin. "You gonna behave and do as I say?"

"I thought we were going to talk."

"We will. After." He met my eyes. "Make a choice, baby."

"How do you know about ropes?"

"Dated a girl who put herself through college as a dominatrix. Now answer the goddamn question."

I shivered. "Let's start with spread eagle."

"Take off your clothes and get on your back," he ordered, and I did as he said immediately.

Once in position, he tied one ankle, then the other before securing them to each bed post. I had to scoot my body down the mattress a little to give him a more slack, but once I did that, I was tied tightly, but not painfully. "You okay?" he asked.

"I'm good," I promised.

Shep moved to my left wrist next, kissing it gently before tying me to the headboard, then he kissed me gently before finally securing my right arm. "Too tight?"

I shook my head.

"We won't have a safe word. If you want to stop, you just say stop, okay?"

"Okay."

"You want toys?" he asked.

"Jesus, you have toys?" I hissed.

"Yes, Lina, I have toys. This ain't my first rodeo."

I scowled, jealously rising out of nowhere. "Just how many women have you brought here?"

"Easy, beautiful." He smiled, leaning down to draw a nipple into his mouth. "Since I haven't lived here long, none. But I've 'played' before, so have a nice selection of toys. So, do you want to play, Lina?"

I arched into his mouth as he moved to my other nipple. "Yes, I'd like to play."

"Hard or soft?"

I swallowed. "Both."

He grinned, kissing me quickly before disappearing back into his closet for a few minutes. If I hadn't been so horny, I might have laughed. Here I was buck-naked, spread-eagle on the man's bed, and he was in his closet, 'shopping' for ways to torture me. The thought made me almost come.

I closed my eyes and took a few deep, steely breaths, when suddenly something whispered over my skin. I opened my eyes and Shep was standing above me with a flogger, running it across my stomach. I tried to squirm, but because I was tied, I had limited mobility. He flicked his wrist, the bite of the suede hitting my belly and I arched with a mew.

He moved it down my thigh, giving it another

flick and I cried out again, my pussy flooding with each sting but when the flogger hit my breasts, I could barely control myself and tugged at my binds as my nipples beaded tight and goosebumps formed all over my body. It was absolute sweet agony, and I didn't want it to end.

After one more slap to my breasts, he tossed the flogger aside and climbed onto the bed, his mouth moving to my neck, then traveling down my body. His tongue swirled around a nipple while his fingers tormented the other and then he bit down gently, and I cried out as my pussy contracted with need.

I couldn't move and I desperately wanted to touch him as he traveled further down my body, his tongue dipping into my navel. I tugged desperately on my binds, arching into his touch as he continued down, and then he was between my thighs and his mouth was on me. Sucking, nibbling, eating, his tongue fucking me before he added his fingers, and I almost felt as though I couldn't take anymore before he pressed his thumb to my clit, and I exploded around his hand.

"Shep!" I screamed, and then all of a sudden, my legs were released, my knees were pushed up to my hips, I think I heard the faint tear of foil before he was inside of me.

"This isn't gonna last long," he warned, burying himself to the hilt. "You good?"

"So fucking good."

He slammed into me… hard. And I almost combusted right then and there, but I refused to let myself go too soon. I wanted to enjoy this a little longer. Jesus, a man who knew how to push my limits was worth his weight in gold.

He placed his hands on each side of me, anchoring himself to the bed, and thrust into me, harder and harder, faster and faster, and the only thing I could do was wrap my legs around his waist. My breasts bounced as he slammed into me, and I arched into him as another orgasm built.

"Shep, please," I rasped.

"Wait," he growled.

"I can't."

He slid out. "Fucking." Then slammed back in. "Wait."

I cried out, "Shep!"

Back out. "You."

In. "Come."

Out. "When."

In. "I."

Out. "Say."

In. "You."

Out. "Come."

"Arrgh," I cried.

In. "Now, Lina."

I exploded and Shep buried his face in my neck as his dick pulsed inside of me. He gently pulled out, then released me from my bonds, tenderly rubbing my arms and kissing me before heading into his bathroom to clean up.

He returned with a washcloth for me, then stretched out beside me and pulled me close. "Are you okay?"

"Never better," I said. "That was amazing."

He chuckled. "Yeah."

"I'd like that on the menu again, please, Chef."

"Oh, are we doing this again?" he challenged.

"Don't be a dick," I sassed. "I like this with you."

"No shit."

"And I've never fucked Clarke."

His body locked. "Do you want to?"

"Again, none of your business."

He leaned up on his elbow with a scowl. "Goddamn it, woman—"

"Oh, calm your tits, Shepard," I snapped, squeezing his face. "No, I don't want to fuck Andrew Clarke. He's helping me with a project and that's all I'm going to say about that."

"Well, he sure as hell wants to fuck you."

"There are a lot of men who want to fuck me, Shep. He can get in line with the rest of them."

He rolled on his back and dragged his hands down his face. "Jesus."

I slid off the mattress and snagged my clothes off the floor. "You need to grow up, buddy. You're a great fucking lay, but you don't own me."

He let out a strangled grunt. "Bullshit."

"What's that supposed to mean?" I asked as I shimmied on my panties.

He knifed off the bed and stalked toward me, yanking my shirt out of my hands and cupping my face. "You stand there and act so fuckin' unaffected by this, but you're in just as deep as me."

I couldn't continue to look at him because I didn't want him to see the truth in my eyes.

"Yeah, exactly," he said.

"This wasn't the deal," I whispered.

"Well, I'm renegotiating."

"I don't want to renegotiate."

"Do me the courtesy of looking at me when you lie to me, Lina."

I let out a frustrated squeak and pulled away from his touch. "Stop it."

"Stop what?"

"Stop looking into my soul. It's annoying."

"What would you rather I do?" he asked. "Fuck you or feed you?"

"Are those my only two options?"

"For the moment, yeah."

I bit my lip. "Feed me then fuck me, I guess."

"Excellent decision, Ms. Monroe."

He leaned down to kiss me, and then handed me back my shirt.

* * *

Shep

I watched Evangeline war with her emotions and smiled. She was telling lies, and I didn't mean the kind she thought she was telling everyone but me. I was talking about the ones she was telling herself.

"What?" she snapped, as she pulled her shirt over her head.

"Nothing, baby. Just like lookin' at ya."

"Stop being weird."

I raised an eyebrow. "You sure you don't need more of what I just did, Lina?"

Her nostrils flared and her face flushed as she swallowed. "Later."

I slid my hand to her neck and stroked her pulse. "Once you eat, we're gonna talk."

"I don't know what you expect from me."

"I only expect the truth."

"I have never lied to you, Shep."

"Lies by omission count as lies, beautiful."

She wrinkled her nose, but dropped her gaze, which was a huge tell, and I kissed her nose.

"Meet me in the kitchen," I said, and after pulling on a pair of sweats and a T-shirt, I left her to her thoughts.

By the time she walked out, I already had pasta on to boil and shrimp in the pan, and she looked a little more composed. She was also wearing one of my hoodies.

"Shrimp scampi good?" I asked.

She slid her hands into the pockets of my sweatshirt. "Yes, it's great, thanks."

I held my arm out. "Come here, baby."

"I'm good here, Shep."

I waved my arm and she let out a quiet huff, but stepped over to me and I wrapped her in a hug. "Tell me why you're pissed off."

"I'm not pissed off."

"Oh, I'm sorry. My mistake." I kissed her temple. "Would you like wine?"

"I'm not pissed off."

"You said that."

She let out a frustrated groan. "Stop it."

"Stop what? I just asked if you wanted wine."

"That's not what you're doing."

"It's not?"

"No, it's not and you know it."

I gave her a squeeze. "Enlighten me, beautiful."

"You're peering into my soul and it's—"

"Pissing you off?" I finished for her.

"No, that's not what's pissing me off."

"But you're pissed about something," I deduced.

"Okay, fine," she snapped, pulling away. "Yes. I guess I am."

"Fill me in, so we can talk it out."

She palmed her eye sockets, then crossed her arms and shook her head.

"Baby, I can't help if you don't talk to me."

"I don't know how I could have possibly let this happen, and you're probably going to dump me once I say it but, I'm in love with you. Okay?" She threw her arms in the air. "Are you happy?"

I chuckled. "Exceedingly."

"Don't be a dick."

I laid a hand on my chest. "I'm a dick because I'm exceedingly happy that the woman I'm in love with is also in love with me?"

"You're a dick because you're smug."

I grinned, wrapping my arms around her and slid my hands to her ass. "I'm smug because I've known you've been in love with me for a while and you've been fighting it. Not sure why, though."

"Because you don't know all my secrets, Shep. And once I tell you, you're going to hate me."

"That's never going to happen."

She dropped her head to my chest and sighed. "I

wish that were true."

"Well, then how about we start at the beginning?"

"Okay, but some other time. Right now, I just want to be here, with you."

"I can so get behind that," I breathed out, holding her close. "But I gotta let you go so I don't burn the shrimp. You wanna open that wine?"

"Yeah, I'll do that."

She grinned up at me and went about opening the bottle.

Seventeen

Shep

THE NEXT MORNING, I had a nine o' clock meeting with my accountant, whose office was near Sylvan Park. I was running ten minutes behind and in such a rush, I almost missed Andrew Clarke. He was sitting in his car, which was parked on the street outside my house.

Clarke climbed out as I approached.

"What the fuck are you doing here?" I asked.

"Cool your jets, cookie, I just want to talk," Clarke replied.

"Look, Evangeline isn't here, I don't know who the fuck you are, and I don't want to, so why don't you get the fuck outta here before I call the cops."

Clarke pulled out a gold star badge and held it up. "That's who I am. You get it now? I *am* the fucking cops."

"You're a long way from Kentucky aren't you, Sheriff?" I asked.

"She didn't tell you, did she?"

I crossed my arms. "What? That you're an asshole? No, she told me that, but I'm pretty sure I could have figured that out myself."

"She didn't tell you that I'm law enforcement."

"Honestly, before the other night at the restaurant, I had no idea you existed. Damn, I was so much happier back then."

"I'm here to warn you. Stay away from Evangeline Monroe."

"Why? Because you think she belongs to you?"

"No. You need to stay away for your own well-being."

"Oh, I'm pretty sure I can look after myself. Plus, anything I can't tend to on my own, Evangeline is perfectly capable to taking care of for me."

"Aren't you curious as to why a sheriff is keeping tabs on your girlfriend?"

"I don't know. The wi-fi in your building is too weak to watch internet porn?"

"I'd be very careful with that smart mouth of yours, Shepard."

I took a step towards him. "Get this straight, Johnny Law. You're out of your juris*dick*tion, and way too close to my house for you to tell me what I will and will not do."

"Alright, alright, tough guy," Clarke said, backing up. "Just do yourself a favor and ask Evangeline about her old friend Reggie. Ask her if she's run into him lately." He chuckled. "I mean, she ran into *someone* to get that shiner, right?"

"I have someplace I've gotta be." I jabbed a finger toward him. "You better not fucking be here, or anywhere else near me when I get back."

"Careful, Chef. That sounded a little like a threat."

"Then let me make myself clearer. If I see your face again, I'm going to punch it. How's that for a threat?"

"Don't forget to ask her."

I turned and walked to my truck, leaving Clarke where he belonged, by the curb, with all the other trash.

* * *

Evangeline

I opened the hotel door and Shep stormed inside.

"Who the fuck is Reggie?" he asked.

"What are you talking about?"

"Your friendly acquaintance was waiting for me outside my house this morning."

"What? Clarke was at your house? Why?"

"To warn me away from you."

"You're kidding. What did he say?"

"He told me to ask you about Reggie and how you really got that black eye."

"I told you that I ran into a—"

"A door, yeah, you told me that. So, what is this about some guy named Reggie?"

"I have no idea. Clarke is crazy. You saw him the other night. He's always wound up."

"Not too crazy to be a cop though, right? A sheriff none-the-less."

"Shep, I—"

"Why didn't you tell me? Why did you lie and tell me Clarke was an old friend?" he demanded.

"There are some chapters of my life that aren't exactly closed. Clarke is part of one of those."

"So, why not just tell me that?"

"Because I'm ashamed of some of the things I've had to do in order to survive. And because you're the best thing that's happened to me in a really long time, maybe ever, and I don't want to drag you into my messy past."

"Messy I can do. Hell, I'll get downright filthy with you, but I can't have you withhold anything important as whatever it is you're going through with this cop. He's bad fucking news. I can feel it."

"I can handle him, you just have to trust me," I said.

"And you promise you don't know anything about a guy named Reggie?"

I shook my head and lied right to his face. It was the first time in my life that telling a lie felt bad. A deep, dull ache in center of my chest burned as I deceived the man I loved.

He sighed. "Why do I feel like you're not telling me something."

"Because Clarke wound you up," I said. "He's a

master of doing that. But let me wind you up another way.”

“What did you have in mind?”

“Get naked and I’ll show you.”

He didn’t hesitate, stripping out of everything and standing before me like a Greek god.

I did the same but left my panties.

I settled a palm in the middle of his chest and spread my fingers. His golden brown skin was smoother than I expected, the light dusting of chest hair soft to the touch as I slid my fingers through it. “You are exquisite.”

“Thank you,” he said with a chuckle.

I ran my finger over a raised scar on his side and met his eyes. “Can I ask what happened here?”

“Got hit by a falling beam in a house fire. Tore through my suit. Nasty cut. Three busted ribs, a punctured lung, and twenty-seven stitches.”

I moved my hands over his pecs, noticing his nipples pebbling, and I leaned in and kissed his chest. He smelled amazing. Like soap and musk. It was heady.

“Is this okay?” I asked.

“Yeah,” he said, but it came out a little strangled.

I looked up at him. “Are you sure, because you sound like you’re chewing glass.”

“I’m good, baby, keep going.”

I continued my exploration, moving to his back, running my fingers over a few more scars across that he explained came from work-related injuries. I kissed each one, and then made my way back to stand in front of him again. “You might be the best looking human I've ever seen," I declared.

Shep chuckled, shaking his head. "You haven't seen a lot of people I take it."

I wrinkled my nose and settled my hands on my hips. "If this is going to work, Shepard Waller, you're going to have to obey me in all things including accepting my compliments when I tell you how handsome you are, got it?"

"My apologies, Ms. Monroe," he said, the sexy smirk back on his face. "Obey you in all things… check. What would you like me to do now, madam?"

"I'm going to kneel in front of you and suck you off," I announced. "And you're not going to interrupt me.

I watched his Adam's apple bob as he swallowed and gave me a quick nod.

I kissed him first then ran my tongue across his chest, biting his nipples gently, smiling as goosebumps formed on his body, and his fists clenched at his sides. I knelt before him, sliding my tongue along his already hard length, before wrapping my lips around him, drawing him deep.

I sucked, licked, worked his balls with my hand, and jacked his dick with my other hand in conjunction with my mouth, taking him so deep my eyes watered. Shep slid his hands into my hair and gripped my scalp, moving his hips and fucking my face and I couldn't figure out who got off on this more, but I'd venture a guess it was me.

"I'm gonna come, Lina," he warned.

I gripped his thighs and pulled him too me, continuing to take him deep, a silent plea to do just that.

Another couple of thrusts and warmth slid down my throat, and I continued to stroke him as I milked him dry.

He stroked my cheek and smiled, once I'd released his cock, continuing to kneel in front of him. "Jesus, Lina, that was incredible."

I ran my tongue over my top lip. "Tasty to the last drop."

He helped me to my feet, kissing me gently as he slid his hand under the waistband of my panties and between my legs. "Soaked."

I gripped his arms with a gasp. "Yeah, that really turned me on."

He dragged a finger through my wet, then pressed it against my clit. "You need some relief, baby?"

Before I could answer, he slid two fingers inside of me, his thumb pressing against my clit with enough pressure, I could barely breathe.

"Panties off, Lina," he ordered, pulling his hand away, and I slid them down my hips immediately. "What do you want?"

"I want you to make love to me."

He slid his hand to my neck and covered my lips with his, kissing me gently. "You want soft, baby?"

"Yeah," I whispered.

He obliged.

* * *

Two hours later, Shep had jumped into the shower while I ordered room service. I'd flipped on the television while we waited for the food and I turned the volume down low.

"In national news, a statewide manhunt is underway for a suspect in the gruesome killing of a Detroit man. Thirty-six-year-old Reginald White, also known as Reggie White, was found stabbed to death in a motel bathtub early Sunday morning by one of the motel's staff members. His body had been badly mutilated, and it appears as though he was tortured before he was killed. Investigators have stated that Reginald White was known to employ sex workers and had accounts with several on-line escort services. Police are asking for cooperation from the public with the assistance of identifying the person or person's responsible for this heinous crime. In local news, the Grand Ol' Opry celebrated its—"

I turned off the TV, but I was too late. Shep was leaning against the open door of the bathroom, a towel wrapped around his waist and the look on his face broke my heart.

Fear. Panic. Pain.

These were the things I wanted to see in my victim's eyes.

Not his.

"Holy shit. You killed him," he said. "Reginald White is the Reggie Clarke was talking about."

"I can explain this, Shep," I rushed to say. "But I need you to stay calm right now."

"You did it, didn't you? That's why Clarke's been hanging around. You're a suspect, aren't you?"

"Shep, if you'd just let me—"

"You lied to me," he said, dressing quickly. "You told me you had no idea who Reggie was. That you had no fucking clue what Clarke was talking about."

"I misled you. You're right. But you need to know I had my reasons."

He dragged his hands down his face. "You fucking lied to me."

"I had to protect myself."

"I would have protected you."

Shep's words broke my heart.

Tears filled my eyes. "I'm sorry."

"When the cops figure out what you've done, they're gonna think I helped you."

"They're not going to find me."

"This small-town sheriff did!"

"Clarke is different," I said.

"Different how? Different from other cops, because I highly doubt that. I mean, do you even know how much he knows about your involvement in Reggie's death?"

I nodded. "He knows all of it."

"All of it?" Shep shouted. "You're telling me that a sheriff knows that you're responsible for murder and you're not in cuffs?"

I took Shep's hands in mine. "Sit down, please."

"Don't tell me to sit down or calm down. You fucking killed a man and you're acting like it's no big deal."

"Shep, honey," I said, cupping his face. "I love you and I really need you to sit down with me and listen to what I have to say."

Finally, Shep took a deep breath and relented. Taking a seat in the chair next to the bed.

"First of all, I want you to know that you're not in danger," I said, sitting on the edge of the mattress. "Not from me or the police. Clarke knows it was me who killed Reggie and that you had nothing to do with it. He hasn't arrested me because he knows the killing was justified."

Shep's face scrunched up in horror. "What the fuck is that supposed to mean?"

"It means that Reggie was one of the men who victimized me. One of the many perverts and pedophiles whose sins have gone unpunished for too long. Clarke has seen men like him skate through life, hiding behind greedy lawyers and corrupt judges. Like me, Clarke understands that the system will always be tilted in favor of men like Reggie. He has no intention of reporting me to anyone. Believe me."

"He's in love with you."

"If I've done my job correctly, yes."

Shep's eyes dropped "Jesus, what a fucking fool I've been."

I waved my hands, frantically. "No, no. It's not the same with you."

"The hell it isn't. You've played me from the very beginning. What was I to you, an alibi? Someone to help you get rid of a body?" The color drained from Shep's face, and his expression turned from fear to dread. "Or maybe you've done this before and—Jesus. You've done this before. Murder."

I nodded.

“A lot of times,” he rasped.

I nodded again.

“Serial killer.”

I grimaced. “I hate labels, but technically, yes.”

I pulled my robe up over my thigh, revealing my butterflies.

“I wondered about those,” Shep said softly.

“One for every kill,” I disclosed.

Eighteen

Shep

"**S**O, THIS IS what you do? Seduce men into helping you get away with murder?"

"No, Shep, I told you. None of this was planned. I mean, meeting you was never in my plans, but the way I feel about you is *real*."

"And what about Clarke?"

She frowned. "What about him?"

"Don't fucking do that," I snapped. "You know what I mean."

I probably should have been afraid of her. Evangeline had just admitted to committing multiple murders. I hadn't studied her tattoo long enough to count the number of butterflies, but I knew it was a high enough number to buy a first-class ticket to the gas chamber.

The fucked up, crazy part, was I wasn't afraid of her. I was completely in love with her and all I wanted to do was protect her. I was terrified of what she'd done and that she'd be caught and taken away from me, but I wasn't scared of *her* or of what she might do to me now that I knew her secret. I'm not exactly sure why. Maybe, it was because I knew deep in my heart that Lina truly loved me the way I loved her.

Or maybe I was just a total dumb shit.

I was leaning more toward dumb shit, mostly because I was smart enough to know that men did a lot of things for pussy. Men were led around by their dicks every day, and I did not think so highly of myself to believe that I could not be fooled into believing that Evangeline could and probably would lie to and manipulate me. Hell, she already had.

On the flipside, I had been a first responder for longer than a decade and I'd seen true evil. Like, fucked up, devil kinda shit, and she wasn't that.

Again, could the argument be made that her magical pussy was making me feel that way?

Maybe.

But somebody who'd been victimized the way that she had couldn't help but lean on her ability to lie and manipulate. It was her defense mechanism, and she had the right to use it. Anyone in her position would surely fantasize about exacting revenge on their abuser. Hell, I responded to a call where an executive assistant had stabbed another assistant with a pair of scissors because she called her a bitch and HR didn't fire her. If thoughts of killing people who pissed us off weren't a thing, road rage wouldn't exist.

The abuse Evangeline, and others like her, suffered were rarely dealt with at a level they probably should be, so she was simply taking care of that. Maybe I was justifying things, and what she was doing certainly wasn't 'right,' but I couldn't necessarily say they were wrong either and I sure as hell wasn't about to play judge and jury. My job, as I saw it, was to protect her.

"Listen, Shep. I'm telling you the truth. I'm using Clarke. I have no other choice. He figured out my connection to some cases on the east coast and confronted me."

I crossed my arms. "But he hasn't turned you in because you're fucking him."

Evangeline's face dropped and I knew at that instant that I'd cut her deep. And that maybe I'd been wrong. "Lina, I'm sorry—"

"No." She held up a hand. "It's okay. I earned that."

"Fuck. That's not true."

"Shep, I just told you that I've committed multiple murders, and here you are trying to apologize for being insensitive."

"I'm scared for you," I said, taking her hand.

"I'm not fucking Clarke. I told you I wasn't, but I also told you I got the black eye from a door, so if I lied about one thing, I can understand why you'd think I'd lie about that."

"It's doesn't matter."

"Of course it matters," she replied. "It matters to me. I may have been treated like a whore my whole life, but who I sleep with and why is a big fucking deal to me.”

“But he’s in love with you?”

She grimaced. “I don’t think Clarke knows what love is. He says he wants to help me.”

“Help you how?”

“He wants to join me. Help me track and execute sickos all around this great land of ours. He’s dreamed up some vigilante lover’s fantasy. Natural Born Killers kind of shit.”

“You’re kidding me.”

“He was obsessed with this case and now he’s obsessed with me.” She sighed. “So, love? No, I don’t think so. He might think he’s in love with me, but it’s really some kind of sick obsession.”

“What are you going to do about him?”

“I haven’t figured that out just yet, but when I do, you’ll be the first to know.” She bit her lip. “If you’re still around that is.”

Something in Evangeline’s voice told me how vulnerable she was.

I stood, stepping over to her and cupping her face. “I’m not going anywhere, but we have clearly got a lot of shit we need to discuss and figure out.”

“I promise I’ll tell you everything. Anything you want to know.”

I lifted her chin and asked, “How many people have you killed?”

“Nine,” she replied.

“Who was your first?”

“Remember the guy I told you about? The one who I drugged and robbed the night I escaped?”

I nodded.

"His name was Bruce Claussen. He owned a bunch of brake shops across the South. The guy was a total slimeball. Anyway, a few years later, I ran into a hustler kid named Scrawny Mike I knew from back then and he told me that Bruce Claussen overdosed on opiates that night. The police thought it was a suicide."

He cocked his head. "So, you never meant to kill him."

"Not him." She shook her head. "Not that time. But every other kill since has been my decision. With Bruce Claussen, I found out so long after the fact that it didn't even help bring closure at the time."

"And the other killings do?"

She bit her lip and nodded. "It's the main reason I do what I do."

"But not the only reason."

Evangeline shook her head. "Torturing and killing them is only the first part. That part is about justice and retribution. That's for me. Disfiguring them and leaving them out in the open to be found is done in service to others."

I took her hands and squeezed them, meeting her eyes. "Why?"

"Because I want the world to finally see who these men truly are. Twisted, grotesque, and vile. Men who have been spit out of the bowels of hell before returning to it, forever."

I frowned. "These men had families."

"Enablers and fools who are better off without

these predators in their lives. At least I give the families the peace of knowing what happened to these sick bastards. If I did the smart thing and disposed of the bodies, they'd spend the rest of their lives wondering why these guys up and disappeared. That's even more cruel if you ask me."

"So, who was the first guy you killed on purpose?"

She shook her head. "Not a guy. It was my mother."

"Jesus Christ," I hissed.

"You have to believe me when I tell you she deserved death most of all. She was the one who first threw me to these wolves like a piece of meat."

"She was still your mother."

"She was my pimp and killing her set me free. She was already dying of bladder cancer and wasn't expected to live more than a year, but I was more than happy to send her to hell a little early."

"How did you do it?"

"I pushed an air bubble into her IV tube via an empty syringe. Her death looked like an old lady dying of a stroke."

"Baby," he rasped.

"I made sure she was awake and alert before I did it and I looked her right in the eyes when I told her what I was doing. I wanted her to know that it was my vengeance coursing through her veins. That she didn't break me and that I was the one sending her to her doom. Once I'd killed her, I knew I could do it again. I'd already damned my soul to hell, so why not?"

"My God."

"You think I'm a monster."

"I think you've suffered unimaginable trauma and that I'm in no way qualified to handle this shit."

"Don't say that. Don't talk to me like some psychiatrist who's afraid to take me on as a patient. I'm me. You know exactly who I am."

"How the hell can you say that, when I just found out you're a fucking serial killer?"

"That's not who I am, it's what I do."

"You don't really think an argument like that is gonna work on me, do you?"

"No, what I think is that I don't have to argue with you at all or justify anything I do. I'm ridding the world of people who victimize children. I'm doing what the cops, churches, and courts refuse to do."

"You keep talking in the present tense. You're not done, are you?"

"I'm not even close."

"Goddammit, Lina. Someone's gonna figure out that it was you behind all these murders. Clarke did."

"He only knows about some of them, and like I said, I've got him under control."

"For now, but what if he decides to talk. Or writes a book? Jesus. An obsessed, lovesick, small-town sheriff doesn't sound like good news to me."

"It's worse than that," she said.

"What?" I asked, terrified of her response.

"He used to be an NYPD homicide detective."

"That's just great," I snapped. "I tell you that's fan-fucking-tastic."

"You know what?" she whispered. "You're right. This is all too much. I'm going to ask you to go."

"Are you fuckin' serious right now?" I snapped, but she'd already shut down.

"I just ask that you say nothing to anyone, okay?"

"Jesus, Lina, I would never betray you, you should know that by now."

"Please, Shep. Just go."

With one last glance, I grabbed my wallet and keys and walked out the door.

* * *

Evangeline

I was lucid enough to walk to the door and lock it, then I slid to the floor, raising my knees to my chest and bursting into tears.

I let myself grieve for about six minutes and then the internal berating began. I had no business falling in love, least of all falling in love with a saint like Shepard Waller. I don't know what the hell I was thinking.

I wasn't thinking, obviously.

But the sad truth was, I *was* in love with him. Completely.

So much so, I actually wanted to give up my 'projects.'

The second I saw his face, my desire to enact justice on my past abusers seemed to wane because Shep eased the pain of that abuse. He was the balm to the wound left behind. I knew he saw me, truly saw me, and I believed him when he said he loved me.

Men said that to me all the time but when Shep said it, it was different. His love wasn't lustful, it was restorative.

And I loved him back. Loved him with the innocence that was lost as a little girl, but also with the knowing of the woman I'd become. And I loved him with everything in between. He was my friend, he was my lover, and I liked him. I wanted to be around him.

I shook my head and stared at the fleur de lis wallpaper.

I couldn't be with him. It wouldn't be right.

He'd become an accessory and even if I gave up everything now, he was still in danger of prosecution because he knew everything I'd done and wasn't going to the police.

I hoped.

I bit my lip. He wouldn't.

I knew that in my soul.

I could trust him.

I burst into tears again, the pain in my chest unbearable.

I'd never been able to trust anyone before.

Not even Mouse.

I mean, maybe I *could* trust Emory, but I would never tell her anything because I wanted to protect her and Papillon House, but with Shep, I knew he could protect himself.

And me.

I let out a deep sigh and hauled my butt up off the floor. I wouldn't ask him to do that. I had no choice but to accept Clarke's terms.

Nineteen

Shep

AT ELEVEN THE next morning, my doorbell pealed in the silence, and I nabbed my cell phone off the nightstand. Checking the screen, I dropped my head and sighed.

Evangeline glanced around, then leaned into the camera. "Shep? Are you home? Please open the door."

I stood next to my bed for a few seconds debating whether or not I was gonna do that when she rang the doorbell again.

"Please, Shep. I just need *one* minute."

I let out a series of curses as I headed to the door and pulled it open, my arm high on the door to keep it

cracked. "You were pretty fuckin' clear about where—
"

"I know," she said, interrupting me by ducking under my arm and forcing her way in. "I'm an idiot, remember?"

"Lina, you're not an idiot." I swung the door shut and crossed my arms facing her. "What are you doing here?"

"I miss you," she whispered, setting her purse on my floor and heading toward my bedroom.

"Where the fuck are you going?" I bit out in frustration.

She didn't answer me as she dropped her T-shirt on the floor and kept walking. Her shoes were next, then her socks.

"Lina."

She continued to ignore me and disappeared into my bedroom.

Jesus, fuck.

I didn't follow for several minutes, mostly because I knew that the second I walked in there, I'd be lost. No, I stood in the hallway and warred with my emotions like a coward. Jesus, fucking Christ, this woman. This woman would be my undoing.

"Evangeline, you need to go."

"Well, I'm not doing that, Shep," she called out.

I dropped my head and studied my feet.

Jesus, fuck.

I forced my legs to move and made my way into the bedroom, stalling to find Evangeline naked on my bed.

Fuck.

"Baby, you really need to—"

"Go. I know," she sassed. "I heard you. But I'm not going to, so let that go, handsome."

"What do you want?" I rasped.

"Well, first, I want to apologize. Then, I want you to fuck me, and then I want to apologize some more. Maybe after that I'll have a look at what's in your fridge and cook for you for a change."

I dropped my head back and stared at my ceiling.

"Please?" she begged.

At that plea, I could no longer keep my resolve, removing my clothes and settling myself between her legs, burying my face in her pussy. Jesus, honey. Absolute paradise. She wrapped her legs around my head, drawing me deeper and I ate her, sucking her clit hard, fucking her with my tongue, then my fingers.

She panted and bucked under my mouth, and it didn't take her long before she was writhing, gasping, her fingers gripping my hair, her moans breaking the silence as she started to come. I didn't wait for her to fully enjoy that climax, flipping her over and smacking her ass. "Get on your knees, Evangeline."

She let out a quiet mew and her body broke out in goosebumps, but she complied immediately.

Fuck.

Yes.

This woman.

She settled her cheek to the bed, raising her hips, baring her pussy and I swallowed, recalling a few hockey stats in order to keep from completely losing my load as I grabbed my cock with one hand and her hip with the other. "Spread your goddamn legs, Lina."

She shivered but I didn't miss her smile as she spread her legs and then I drove in, watching her pussy take me, burying myself to the hilt. I closed my eyes, the ecstasy of her warm, wet heat nearly my undoing.

"Fuck me, Shep," she begged, and I lost my resolve.

I set a hand on the bed beside her and curled my body around her, grasping her hip for leverage and did just that.

I fucked her fast and deep, harder and harder, my face in her hair, giving her one more orgasm before I bit out, "Touch yourself, Lina."

Fucking hell, her hair smelled like mint.

I buried myself deeper (if that was possible), moving my hand to her breast, twisting her nipple, hard, as she worked her clit.

"Jesus, you have the best tits," I breathed out as I watched them bounce as she slammed herself back onto my dick.

"Well, I'm kind of a fan of your dick," she said, then cried out as another orgasm hit. "Oh my god, that's three."

"I'm aware," I grunted out.

"Your turn, Shep."

"You gonna keep takin' it, Lina?"

"Hell yes."

"How do you want it?"

"I want to ride you," she panted out.

I kissed her shoulder, and pulled out, dropping onto my back. "Climb on, beautiful."

She licked her lips and straddled me, reaching between her legs and gripping my cock, guiding me to her entrance.

"Fuck."

"Shit, did I hurt you?" she asked.

"No." I slid my hands to her ass. "Just holdin' on by a thread here."

She settled her hands on my chest and smiled. "Let it go, honey."

"When you come again, I'll come."

"So I'm forgiven, then?" she asked, hopefully.

"This is your goodbye fuck, Evangeline."

"No," she snapped, rising up, then impaling herself, her eyes meeting mine.

"Lina—"

"Don't," she bossed, narrowing her eyes, but not looking away. "If you speak, I'll lose my nerve."

"Jesus, we don't have to do this."

"Shut. Up," she hissed, grinding down on me, still looking at me.

"Baby," I breathed out, and her eyes filled with tears.

She still did not look away.

"Enough," I demanded, flipping her onto her back.

"Shep!" she admonished.

"We're not ending it this way."

"I don't want to end it at all."

"That's not what you said yesterday."

She closed her eyes, tears sliding down her temples. "Like I said, I'm an idiot."

"You call yourself an idiot one more time, Evangeline, I'm gonna lose my shit."

"When it comes to you, I turn into one." She settled her fingers over my mouth before I could say anything and sighed. "Just let me get this out, honey, please."

I raised an eyebrow but nodded.

"You scare me. Not because I'm afraid of you but because you treat me with respect, and I can't get around you. When men, or anyone for that matter, find out what I've been through, they treat me like a delicate China doll. You treat me like a peer. And you're amazing in bed."

I wiped the tears from her temples. "You are too, Lina."

"I'm not angling for compliments here, Shep. I'm trying to tell you why I freaked out on you."

"I already know why."

She flapped her arms around me. "Why?"

"Because you're trying to push me away before you let me in more. If you do that, you might get hurt. So, if you act the fool with all your nonsense and shenanigans and push me away, then you're the one making all the decisions, ergo, you're the one doing the hurting. No one gets to hurt you anymore. You made that decision the day you walked out of that life, sweetheart, consciously or not. So when you met me, and I being awesome in every way, and exactly who you need, totally fucked up your plan to keep your defenses up."

"You being awesome in every way?"

"Yep."

"Your dick is still buried inside of me and you're saying that to me?" she demanded.

"Hell, yeah. You want me to pull out?"

Wrinkling her nose, she grumbled, "Well, no."

"Didn't think so." I grinned. "Want me to finish what you started?"

"Are you going to let me cook for you?"

"No."

She gasped. "Are you going to make me leave?"

"No, honey." I ran my nose against hers, then kissed her. "Gonna fuck you again, then I'm gonna cook for you."

She smiled slowly. "Oh, okay."

I kissed her again, then did exactly as I promised.

* * *

Evangeline

Later that night, we were curled up in bed after another momentous fuck session and Shep stroked my thigh. "Tell me about your butterflies."

I nodded. Allowing his hand to gently trace my tattoos. I still couldn't believe how safe I felt when I was in his arms. It was a feeling I could get used to, which of course freaked me out.

"Do you know much about the Monarch butterfly?" I asked.

He shifted slightly and smiled. "I remember doing a class report on them in the sixth grade. Everyone in the class made butterfly cutouts out of orange and black construction paper and paste, then the next day, we came into class to find that our teacher, Miss Bartley, had hung them up from the ceiling. It seemed like there were a thousand of them."

"What a sweet memory," I said. "I wasn't allowed to go to school. At least, not until after I escaped and by then I didn't really see the need. At least until college."

He ran a finger down my cheek. "I'm sorry you never got to experience things like that."

I shrugged.

"For what it's worth, school was mostly made up of monotonous, boring, days of shoveling bullshit with a spoon."

I wrinkled my nose. "That doesn't sound like fun at all."

"It wasn't and I was a shit student, which is why I don't remember anything useful about Monarch butterflies."

I rolled onto my side, facing him. "They are amazing."

He flashed his boyish grin. "Tell me everything."

I cleared my throat and did my best impression of a college professor. "Danaus Plexippus, also known as the Monarch butterfly, named by King William III of England, is a migratory pollinator of the Milk Weed—"

Shep laughed. "Just tell me why they are amazing and why you love them so much."

"Right." I blushed. "They don't start off as anything special. The lifecycle of the Monarch is the same as any other lepidopteran species.”

Shep waved his hand casually. “But of course.”

“It moves from egg, to larva, to pupa, and then finally the adult stage. But Monarchs are different. Tougher, more resilient.”

“Why?”

“Because the planet is filled with predators and parasites. But, the Monarch, as beautiful as she may be, has learned how to evade and defeat them over time.”

He ran his finger gently down my cheek. “Just like you.”

I blushed. “And just like me, the Monarch migrates. Hatching from her cocoon on the east coast of the United States, a month or less from her beginnings as an egg, she flaps her wings and flies off headed west. Guided only by instinct and intuition.”

“How far will she go?”

“As far as the west coast of California and Mexico, and then all the way back again in the spring, but there’s a catch. It won’t be her who makes it all the way there and back. It will be her descendants. The migration path of the Monarch is multi-generational. They stop and breed along the way, often pursued my several potential suitors at any given time. Some making their approach from the sky, while others spring from the ground below.”

“Which suitor wins?”

“Whichever one can pin her down long enough to copulate.”

“Is that so?” He raised an eyebrow. “And how does she evade capture?”

"Through mimicry. Birds, mice, and other predatory insects all find the Monarch quite delicious. In fact, fewer than ten percent of Monarchs even survive past the egg stage. The survival odds of the Monarch are low, but she doesn't give a single fuck. As beautiful as she may be, she's learned how to blend in when necessary. In fact, over time she's even learned how to mimic the far less tasty Viceroy butterfly, who predators know to avoid."

"Sounds like your spirit animal."

I smiled. "Spirit insect, but point taken."

Shep perched up on his elbow. "How do you know all this? I mean, you're legitimately brilliant, but you were never allowed to go to school."

"From as far back as I can remember, I've read just about anything I could get my hands on. As if there was something inside of me compelling me to educate myself. I think I always knew I'd be alone and would have to fend for myself and have tried my best to prepare. Most of the other girls never even tried to escape. At best they'd hope and pray that someone would come and rescue them, but I've never been one for hopes and prayers. I stole, smuggled and hid books every chance I got. Sometimes Sugar's crew would find my stash and I'd get slapped around, but expanding my mind was worth the beating."

"And once you escaped?"

"I already had an excellent fake ID, supplied by Sugar in case I was ever hauled in by the cops, and the first thing I did with it was get a library card. The next thing I got was a gun."

"With a fake ID?"

"The guy I bought the gun from wasn't exactly the type to run a background check, ya know?"

Shep nodded. "So, then what?"

"I knew where the bus station was because Sugar would troll for new girls there. So, I ran all the way there and bought a ticket for the next bus out of town. Twenty three hours later I was in Boston. I got a job in housekeeping at a shitty motel. The kind of place men had taken me all my life. One of the perks being the owner let me stay in the room at the far end of the complex. He never rented that room because it was right next to the dumpsters and guests would complain about the smell and noise. I didn't give a shit. It was free rent, and I knew no one would bother me in a place like this. In fact, it was there at the Sunlight Motor Inn that I realized what my purpose was."

"And what is that?"

"To stop as many men as possible from taking children into places like that any way I could. I would write books, I would give speeches, I would start a home to provide shelter, counseling and legal aid to as many trafficking victims as possible. And, most of all, I would remove as many predators as I possibly could from the face of the earth. I would become vengeance herself. I would strike fear into the hearts of evil men. I would get bloody. I would become death."

"What about Emory? Does she know about all of this?"

I shook my head. "I met Mouse six months after

arriving in Boston. She taught me how to use a computer and I taught her how to use people. We became close quickly, but I've never said a word to her about my projects."

"How come?"

"To protect her. If I'm ever caught, I don't want her connected to my work in any way. The best way for me to keep her safe is to keep her in the dark. That goes for everyone."

"Everyone except me," Shep challenged.

"I never wanted you to know. There was never supposed to be a *you* in the first place."

"You sure know how to make a guy feel special," Shep teased.

"I'm used to being alone. It's where I feel safest. At least it *was* until I met you."

"I was just giving you a hard time, you don't have to—"

I turned to face him. "I mean it, Shep. You're the only person who's ever made me feel safe. You put me at ease the second I met you. I don't know how or why, but something inside me knew that I could trust you. How do you explain that?"

"I can't and I'm not sure I'd even want to try. How do you explain love?"

"Love?"

"Sure. Trust is what love is built out of. To fall in love with someone is to take a trust fall. Blindly falling backwards into the unknown. Hoping the ones we trust will be there to catch us before we hit the ground."

"Shepard Waller, poet chef," I said.

"Is that what I should have the printer put on my next business card?"

I laughed. "Most definitely."

"What about you? What's gonna be on your next card?"

I thought for a moment, then said, "Evangeline Monroe, Exterminator."

"How long do you plan on doing this?" Shep asked.

"Careful."

"What? I think it's a fair question."

"One I wouldn't have to answer if I were alone."

"And I thought we were having a moment."

I sat up. "This is exactly what I was afraid of. I knew the moment I dropped my guard and let you in that the clock would start ticking."

"What are you talking about?"

"You're telling me to stop doing my projects."

"I don't remember telling you to do anything. All I did was ask how long you planned on continuing?"

"Which is the first clock chime. Next time you ask, there will be a big fight. Then the asking will turn to demands, and then we're doomed."

"I can't tell the future, but I can say with one hundred percent certainty that you will never write a script for a Hallmark romance movie."

"I'm being serious, Shep."

"So am I. I love you and I'm scared of losing you. Anything could happen to you out there, from being killed by one of these men to being caught by the police. I mean, think about it. What am I supposed to do while you're out hunting at night? Wait alone at home with my phone in hand?”

“Honestly, I haven’t thought much about what a future with you would look like.”

He grimaced. “Ouch, more brutal truth.”

“This is coming out all wrong. What I’m saying is that I’ve never thought of a future with anyone, *ever*. For exactly these reasons. The only people I’m responsible for are the kids at Papillion House and I want to keep it that way.”

“What do you think will happen to them if you go to prison?”

“They are in the best hands with Emory. She’d take my position and would likely do a better job than me in the end.”

“If Papillion House survived the scandal,” Shep said, his words piercing my heart.

I’d never thought about my actions tarnishing the reputation of our foundation.

“It doesn’t matter, because I’m not going to get caught.”

Shep sighed, cupping my face. “Baby, everyone gets caught eventually.”

“Well, I won’t.” I met his eyes. “Unless someone I love and trust narcs.”

“I’m not gonna tell anyone shit,” he avowed. “But I would like you to seriously consider being done with all of this.”

“I’ll give your words some thought.”

He closed his eyes and took a deep breath. “That sounds vague.”

“That’s the best I can give you.” I wrapped my arms around his waist. “Is that enough?”

"No. But you're enough." He gave me a squeeze. "Is there anything else you'd like to tell me?"

"Yes, there is," I whispered. "I love you and I'm going to figure out how to get us both out of this situation, but I need you to trust me."

"Lina, I don't know how any of this ends without both of us in jail, but if there's a snowball's chance in hell, we make it, I'll try. But there can't be any more secrets and lies."

"I promise," I said.

"Alright, what's the plan?"

Evangeline

$\mathcal{S}$OMETIME AROUND TEN o'clock the next morning, there was a knock on my hotel door, and thinking it was Shep, I raced to open it.

"I didn't expect you to answer so fast," Clarke said.

I tried to slam the door, but Clarke wedged his foot inside the door before I could close it.

"I don't care that you're a cop. Remove your foot, or I swear I'll remove it for you," I hissed.

"Five minutes, that's all I want. You can time me, I swear. Give me five minutes to talk and I'll get back into my car and drive back to Black Sheep Hollow today."

"You stay right there, I stay inside. Five minutes, and the clock is ticking," I said, checking the time.

"I need to know your answer before I go back home," Clarke said.

"You haven't left me with much of a choice, have you?"

"I believe you know what the right thing to do is in the situation. Not for me or even for you, but for all the children you're fighting to protect. Partnering with me is the only way to ensure that you are allowed to continue your work."

"I know," I said, and this time I wasn't lying. Clarke's plan made a lot of sense, and I could work with far more freedom, knowing I had him and his badge to hide behind. I was also confident I'd be able to manipulate Clarke into just about anything, especially once I finally let him have sex with me.

The bottom line was, choosing a life with Shep was selfish and ultimately doomed to fail. It would also likely put an end to my work, as Shep clearly wanted me to stop, and I was afraid that my love for him would eventually cause me to acquiesce.

A life with Clarke meant continuing the work, which was the most important thing. Not just for me, but for all future victims. Clarke was right about that. He was also right, that without someone to help cover my tracks, I would eventually be caught. Choosing a life with Clarke meant working with someone who understands me and the importance of my work. It also meant the avoidance of heartbreak down the line.

"Look, Evangeline. I meant what I said about

taking care of you and protecting you. I'm not trying to push myself on you. I'm trying to pull you to safety."

"You have four minutes left."

"Yeah, but you don't. What's it going to be? Are you going to stay here with the cook? Put down some roots here in Nashville. Have some kids. Wait for the day a couple o' boys in blue show up on the doorstep to arrest you in front of them? Or start a new life with the only man who will ever fully understand you?"

I nodded. "You're right. I know you are and I'm going to go with you, but you need to give me a day to break things off with Shep. Just one more day here in Nashville and then I'll be on a plane back home to Boston. Once you're home in Kentucky we can discuss how our relationship is going to work. Agreed?"

Clarke smiled and nodded. "On all points except one."

"What's that?"

Clarke craned his head into the doorway. "You need to get rid of the cook."

"I told you I'm going to break things off with him right away."

He shook his head. "You *know* what I mean. The cook knows too much. About you, about me. I want him gone for good."

"I don't kill innocent people."

"No one is innocent," Clarke said. "He's a liability. A boy Scout like that will go running to the local cops the minute you dump him. Besides, that's my price for helping you. I want Shepard Waller dead. After that, I'll know I have a partner I can trust."

"Fine, but if you try and alter this deal one more time, I swear on my dead mother's grave, you'll need to dig two holes. One for Shep and one for yourself."

"Once he's out of the picture, we can begin finding you your next target."

"I call them projects, and I work alone. I research and pick my own projects, and do not want or need your help. I will let you know when I'm ready to work again. Until then, go home and wait for me to contact you. You have one minute left."

"Don't worry, I'm leaving, but not before giving you this," he said, reaching into his coat pocket.

"What is it?"

"It's a buttonhole spy cam. One of the smallest on the market."

"What am I supposed to do with it?"

"You're going to conceal it somewhere on yourself, when you're going to kill Shep. It's linked up to a live feed I have running back at my place. So, I'll be able to watch you get rid of Shep in real time while I'm safely one state away with plenty of alibis. All of which happen to be in law enforcement."

"You've really thought of everything haven't you?" I asked.

"I'm telling you. My brains and your beauty are going to keep us safe."

"I hope you're right," I replied before closing the door.

* * *

I told Shep to drive East on I-40 for twenty minutes until we reached Woodland Point. A public use stretch of waterfront land on Priest Lake.

"Jesus, Lina, what the hell are we doing here?" Shep asked as we climbed out of his truck.

"It's beautiful out here, isn't it?" I asked, casually scoping out the area for other people. Happy to find none. I'd vetted the area earlier and found it to be the perfect location unless some nosy hiker happened to stumble upon us.

"I wanted us to talk in private," I said. "Someplace where you could yell at me without drawing attention."

"Why would I yell at you?" Shep asked.

"Let's take a walk over to that bridge. There's something I want to show you," I said, pointing to an area a few hundred feet from where we were standing.

"You've been here before?" Shep asked.

I nodded. "The first time I came to Nashville. I signed at an event held here while on my first book tour."

We reached the small bridge just as the sun was beginning to set. A fitting time of day for what I had to do.

"This bridge was built in 1864, by hand. Isn't that something?"

Once we'd reached the halfway point across the bridge, Shep stopped us and took my hands in his.

"Are you going to explain why we're here, and why you think I'd yell at you?"

"Because I have something to tell you that is going to make you unhappy."

"There's only one thing that could make me unhappy and that's you leaving."

I said nothing.

Shep shook his head. "Lina, don't do this."

"You have to understand why I'm doing this. I have no choice."

"You can't go with him. You can't seriously tell me that you're going to take Clarke's offer."

"I already have," I said, tears streaming down my face.

"No, no, no way," Shep growled, before letting go of my hands. "He's using you, Lina."

"I know he is. That's why I have to go with him."

"What the fuck does that mean?"

"It means that I love you, and that I want you to have a happy life. One devoid of serial killing girlfriends and blackmailing cops. One that ends in 'They lived happily ever after,' not 'I hereby sentence you to…'"

"I promise I'll protect you."

"And I believe you, but *I* can't protect *you*, and a real partner should be able to do that. I don't care what happens to Clarke. He's a means to an end and a current necessary evil. As soon as I can get him out of the picture safely, I will, but until then, he's my best shot at long term survival."

"So, that's it. You've decided we're through and

I just have to deal with it?"

Tears flowed freely now. "I'm so sorry, Shep. We have to say goodbye, right here and now and I need you to promise that you'll never come after me or tell anyone anything about our relationship."

"Lina—"

"This is important, Shep," I said, sharply. "Life or death important. You need to swear you'll stay absolutely quiet about me and Clarke."

Shep nodded.

"And you have to forget about me. The sooner the better."

"I love you, Lina. I can't imagine there ever being a time when I don't feel that way."

I wiped the tears from my eyes and swallowed hard. "I'm going to walk that way, over this bridge, and I need you to turn around and walk the other way to your truck. Get in and drive away."

"What about you?"

"Don't worry about me. I'll call for a car. I just need us to walk away from each other. No goodbyes and no goodbye kisses. We turn and walk. That's the only way I'll know you'll be able to leave me alone."

"That's really the way you want this to end?" Shep asked.

"It is," I said, turning to leave.

I'd only taken two steps when Shep grabbed my hand, spun me around and kissed me so hard I felt it down in my soul.

"I wish you hadn't done that," I whispered softly.

"I will never turn my back on you or let you go," Shep said. "Ever. Do you understand me?"

"I know," I replied, producing the knife hidden in my jacket pocket and thrusting it deep into Shep's abdomen. His back was against the bridge's railing, giving me the leverage I needed to slice his belly wide open. His entrails spilling out onto the bridge's historical planks.

I crouched down, and using all of my strength, grabbed Shep's legs and heaved him over the side of the bridge and into the water below. He thrashed around for twenty seconds or so before either taking in too much water or losing too much blood. Either way, he was gone.

"I hope you're happy now," I said.

I watched Shep's dead body float, motionless, face-down, for five minutes before I made my way down to the water's edge to clean up. Once I was spick and span it was time for Shep's truck, which I cleaned thoroughly with the stash of cleaning products I'd hidden under the passenger seat. I'd also packed a go bag for myself, which included a change of clothes, a fake ID, cash, and a snub-nose 38.

I hiked a few miles before burying the knife I'd used to stab Shep, and then made my way toward the highway where I would call for a ride-share under the cover that I was a stranded motorist whose car had broken down.

It wasn't until I reached my hotel room that I completely lost my shit. Crying, screaming into my pillow, pulling my hair, and cursing Clarke for what he made me do. Cursing Shep for not walking away. If he had just been able to convince me that he'd leave well enough alone then I wouldn't have had to do what I did.

I reached into my go bag and retrieved the spy cam Clarke had me wear and pointed it directly at myself.

"Did you hear what I said back at the lake? I said I hope you're fucking happy now. Shep is dead and his blood is on your hands. And let me make something crystal fucking clear, Clarke. You may have gotten your way, but I will never forgive you for this."

Evangeline

ONCE I'D BEEN back home for a few days and had settled in, I called Clarke. We had a lot to talk about, and I'd have to put my personal feelings aside the best I could if I was going to put him at ease. I shuddered. I knew it had to be done, for the greater good.

"This is a burner phone, so don't worry about traces or recordings," I said, as soon as he accepted the call.

"And hello to you, too, Evangeline. How are you this evening?"

"I'm pissed that's what I am. Shep was an innocent man. A good man, who I happened to care about. You could have let him walk."

"Like you tried to do on that bridge? What the

hell was that all about? I told you to kill the cook not to give him a choice."

I squeezed my eyes shut. "I'd hoped Shep would convince us both that he was willing to walk away and forget about me."

"But he was never going to do that which is why I wanted him out of the picture in the first place."

"I know, I know," I snapped. "You were right, okay. Is that what you want to hear? Shep would have come after me eventually, and who knows who he'd tell to get me to stop. I probably would have had to kill him some other time if not then, but I don't like that it was on your terms."

"That's all behind us," Clarke said. "Now we can focus on the future."

"That's exactly what I want to talk about. First of all, we need to establish a home base, and if you think I'm moving to Beaver Dick Junction, you're out of your fucking mind."

"I suppose you want me to move to Boston?"

"Papillion House is here. I'm set up and established in Boston, and I know there's no way a New York boy such as yourself would rather live in Eastern Kentucky than Boston."

"You do know about the long-standing rivalry between the Yankees and the Red Socks, right?"

"If you ever try to talk to me about sports again, it'll be the last thing you do," I said without a trace of humor in my voice.

"Are you gonna be like this all the time?" Clarke asked.

"What do you want from me? Just because I kill

people doesn't mean I'm a heartless robot. I kill these monsters because I care about the people they hurt. Shepard Waller was not only a good man, but he was an actual hero. I get that he was also a huge liability who would likely have turned me in but forgive me if I'm not throwing a party in his absence."

"I'm sorry, Evangeline. I truly am. I wouldn't have asked you to take care of Shep if I didn't know you were strong enough to handle it."

"So, it's agreed. You'll move to Boston," I said, ignoring Clarke's apology.

"Actually, no. It's not. When I was shitcanned from the NYPD, they made sure word got around via the 'blue wire' that I was damaged goods. Landing the sheriff gig in Black Sheep Hollow was as good as I could get unless I wanted to start from ground zero, shoveling dog shit in a K-9 patrol somewhere. You need me in a ranking law enforcement position if I can be of any real use, so I'm afraid for the foreseeable future, I'm stuck here in the Holler."

"That's why I'm the beauty and the brains of this operation and you're just the badge."

"What's that supposed to mean?"

"It means that I happen to be good friends with the Police Captain of the Hyde Park precinct. A good friend who happens to owe me a few serious favors. One phone call from me and you're all but hired. As long as you don't act like dick when you meet with him, he'll look past any bad press from those New York assholes. Trust me. This is your opportunity to put down the sheriff's star and pick up a detective's shield again."

"I can't just pick up and move to Boston on your word."

"I've done what you've asked, now I need you to trust me. I'll call Captain Townsend tomorrow and see if he'll agree to a preliminary phone interview if that would make you feel better."

"No," Clarke bit out with a huff. "I'm no good on the phone. Interviews need to be face to face. I come across best when I'm in the room. You're right. If we're gonna be partners, I have to learn to trust you. Gimmie a week to get my shit sorted out down here, and to find a place to rent in Boston."

"I thought you could stay here with me, until you get settled in. That way you'd have time to look around and get a feel for the different areas before you rented a place. How does that sound to you?"

"Sounds like Deputy Jost is about to get the promotion of a lifetime. All for the best, really. Everyone in town already knows and likes Jost. Plus, they all think I'm an asshole anyways."

"Put in your notice and tell everyone at the station that you're taking a new job out of state, but don't tell them what it is or where. In fact, the less they know about your exit, the better."

"I read you, loud and clear," Clarke replied. "Scraping the shit that is this town off my shoes will be an absolute pleasure."

"Let me know when you'll be arriving, and I'll have everything ready for you when you get here."

"We're going to do good work together, Evangeline," Clarke said.

"That's all that's important to me," I said before

hanging up.

* * *

Six days later Clarke arrived in Boston. He'd turned in his notice with the sheriff's office and his police union representative the day after we last spoke and was currently on sabbatical until he decided to return to the force. His house in Kentucky was a month-to-month rental, so he had no issues there. He simply packed up his Land Rover and drove fifteen hours from Black Sheep Hollow to Beantown. With no boss, no wife, no friends, no work attachments, and no family to speak of, he was in exactly the position I needed him to be.

"Now that you're here in Boston, I'd like to start from scratch if we can," I said.

"No one would like to put the past in the rearview more than me," Clarke replied.

"Good, because if we can't trust each other, one or both of us could end up in jail or dead."

"I understand and couldn't agree more," Clarke said.

"Okay then. Let's get started," I said, rolling up the metal bay door that led inside.

I'd asked Clarke to meet at our current location as soon as he got into town. I made it clear that I didn't want anyone spotting him until he came here. No gas station attendants, no waitresses, no one. I told him to use his GPS to avoid all toll roads. I wanted him to be a ghost.

"Welcome to my office," I said, as I hit the lights.

"This is your office, huh? It's spacious but I'd hire a decorator if I were you."

"We're going to use this place as our bullpen. If you're going to be my partner, you're going to need to know every detail of how I work. How I research a subject, how I track them, the tools I use, and most importantly how I choose a site." I motioned to the room. "This is exactly the kind of place I like to work. Private, industrial, far from any main roads, and without cameras."

"Are you always so methodical?" he asked, strolling the room.

"Whenever possible," I replied. "But there have been times, take Judge Faulkner for instance, when I had to deviate from my normal routines. I couldn't risk having his death draw too much attention. If his death seemed suspicious in any way, it would only be a matter of time before the police would connect him to George Hanford and Henry Duplass, therefore I had to make look like an accident."

"And a fat, old, drunk guy drowning while on vacation is pretty open and shut," Clarke said. "My god you are brilliant."

"You figured me out," I retorted with a shrug. "And I still don't know how exactly."

"Equal parts hard work, obsession, and dumb luck," Clarke said. "My ex-deputy and newly appointed interim sheriff of Black Sheep Hollow had something to do with it as well."

"Is he going to be a problem for us?"

"Jost? No way," Clarke said, dismissively.

"How can you be so sure? You said it yourself

that he helped track me.”

“I told him you were a dead-end. Nothing left to look into. And besides, he was only working the case at my behest. Neither of us was ever working the case within the NYPD or the Kentucky Sheriff’s Department, so the only records are mine.”

“And where are those?” I asked.

“In the back of my SUV, along with everything else I own. I left most of the shit in my house behind for the next folks, and there wasn’t much.”

“Good,” I said. “So, there’s no one in Kentucky or New York who’ll be sticking their noses in our business?”

“I’m as unattached as a man can be.”

“That’s exactly what I needed to hear before I show you how I operate. Now, there’s only one last thing to take care of.”

“What’s that?” Clarke asked.

“This,” I replied, before injecting him in the neck with a dose of Nightfall.

* * *

Clarke

I have no idea how long I was unconscious, but when I came to, my mouth was bone dry, and my head was pounding. At first, I thought my inability to move my limbs was due to whatever Evangeline hit me with, but soon figured out that I was restrained. Bound to a table, flat on my back.

“Oh, good, you’re awake,” Evangeline said.

“What is this? What are you doing?” I croaked

out.

"I told you. If we're going to be partners, you need to learn about every step of my process."

"Why am I on this table?"

"It would be helpful if you saved your questions until after class is through," Evangeline said.

"Please, cut me loose," I said, full-on panic setting in. "I get the picture. I understand how your victims feel now."

"I told you, they're not victims. They are projects," Evangeline corrected. "I was the victim. In fact, I was *your* victim."

"I'm only here to help you, I told you that. I thought we trusted each other."

"Trust you? Never in a million fucking years would I trust you. You not only forced me to kill the only man I've ever loved, but you made me film it for you. What kind of sick fuck would ask someone to do that? And how arrogant would he have to be to think I'd ever spend one single solitary moment as his partner after that?"

"But, you told me—"

"I told you what you wanted to hear. That we could live together, that there was a job waiting for you here in Boston, that one day, maybe you'd get to put your dirty fucking paws all over me."

"You lying whore," I spat out.

Evangeline laughed. "You're any better? You told me and your deputy that you were working a joint case with the NYPD. That was a lie. You told me all about your family back in the holler. Also, a lie. Every other thing that comes out of your cocky mouth is a lie."

"Why not just kill me? Why make me believe that we were on the same side?"

"Because I needed to make sure that you'd cut all ties in Kentucky before I could get rid of you. I couldn't chance any loose ends, so I had you tie them all up for me before joining me here."

"I can't believe I ever trusted you."

"You really thought you had me under your thumb, didn't you?" Evangeline asked.

I laughed. Hard.

"I am very curious to know what you could possibly find funny at this moment," she asked.

"You want to talk about power over you? Sure, you might be able to kill me, but for the rest of your dumb whore life, you'll know that it was *me* who made you kill that fucking cook."

"You sure about that, city boy?" I heard Shepard Waller ask and turned my head to see him approaching the table.

My blood boiled at the sight of him, very much alive and well.

"I saw you die," I said, hardly believing what I was seeing.

"You saw magic tricks and props courtesy of an old friend. A retractable stage knife, some phony blood and guts, and an air hose hidden under the water that led out to a patch of reeds on the shoreline. That way I could breathe while face down in the water while appearing dead from the surface."

I pulled at my restraints with every ounce of strength I had. "I'm going to fucking kill you both!"

I screamed.

"No, you won't," Evangeline said. "And you won't use me for whatever sick fantasies you had dreamed up for me either. Tonight, you and your abuse will come to an end."

"You can't honestly think that I'm anything like the scum you've killed before," I challenged.

"You're no different than every other man who's ever abused me, and tonight you're going to die like they did. Under my terms. Under my control."

"Shep, come on, man. You're not really gonna let her kill me, are you?"

"I am," he said. "Partly because I think she's dead right about you. About what kind of man you are? You abused your power as an officer of the law, and frankly I just hate your fuckin' guts."

"But also, because I promised him that you're my last project, Clarke," Evangeline said.

I laughed again. "Right. You don't really believe that do you, Shep? Come on man. She's lying to you. Now that she's tasted blood, she won't be able to stop. You gotta know that."

"You're wrong," she said. "You've been wrong about me the whole time, and what's more important, Shep was right. I *don't* need to do this anymore. I'd rather spend my time in the light with Shep, Mouse, and the kids at Papillion House instead of in the dark, hunting monsters like you."

"If that's true, then you can let me go."

* * *

"I told you earlier, if we can't trust each other one of us was going to end up dead. Well, Clarke. I'm afraid I just don't trust you."

I cut Clarke's throat with one, deep, quick cut of my straight razor, having promised Shep that I wouldn't torture him first. Honestly, it was an easy request to grant. I just wanted all of this finished.

Clarke writhed within his restraints. His face draining of color as his eyes turned red.

I put one hand on Clarke's chest and one on his forehead, looking him in the eyes as he gurgled blood, gasping in futility for air that would never reach his lungs.

"Shhhhh. This will all be over soon," I whispered, telling Clarke one final lie. From my experience, I knew it could take up to four or five minutes for a person to die from this type of wound, and I'm not even really sure why I felt the need to comfort him at all.

Maybe it was because, outside of Shep, Clarke was the only other person who knew my secret. The only other person to see the side of myself I kept hidden from the world.

Shep stood back as I stayed with Clarke, comforting him until the final moment of his life passed.

Epilogue

Evangeline

One year later…

"LINA!" SHEP CALLED up the stairs. "We're gonna be late."

"Keep your pants on!" I called back, sliding my shoe on.

"Might I remind you we're late because I took them off to begin with?" he retorted from the doorway of our bedroom.

I wrinkled my nose as I grabbed my purse off the bed and closed the distance between us. "Technically, you dropped them to your ankles."

He chuckled, leaning down to kiss me gently,

stroking my cheek. "You look beautiful."

"Thanks, honey."

"But you need to get your ass in the truck."

"Lead on, big man."

I followed him down the stairs, and out to the garage where he helped me into his truck. We were heading to the Institute of Contemporary Art where I was to be awarded Woman of the Year, which I felt was all a little over the top and ridiculous, but my man was giddy with excitement.

So much had happened over the last year. Once I'd disposed of Clarke, leaving Shep out of that process entirely for plausible deniability, I'd been a little nervous that perhaps someone might come looking for him, but no one did. Despite the fact the sheriff had been a pathological liar, he'd at least told the truth about leaving everything behind, so I had finally been able to relax.

Shep had closed up shop in Nashville, moved to Boston, and married me. He'd insisted that if he was going to move, marriage was non-negotiable. Plus, he'd argued that as my husband, he wouldn't have to testify against me, should my past crimes ever catch up to me.

It really didn't take much to convince me, to be honest. I was stupid in love with him, and how could I say no to the man who'd brought me into the light? The answer was, I couldn't. He'd also figured out a way to help me curb my 'itch.'

It was sex.

The dirtier the better.

So, to say the darkness was being beaten back

with a stick, or a flogger, or a paddle, was an understatement. And a delicious understatement at that.

Shep had started an extremely successful catering business here in Boston, and in his 'down time,' he taught the kids at Papillon House how to cook. They adored him, and it gave them yet another skill to carry with them when they left.

Shep reached over and linked his fingers with mine. "Love you, beautiful."

We had matching butterflies on our wrists with our wedding date, and I gave his hand a squeeze as I smiled. "Love you, too."

For a little girl who had a rough start in life, this man had certainly healed her in ways she could have never imagined. Redemption never felt so good.

New York Times & USA Today Bestselling Author Piper Davenport writes from a place of passion and intrigue, combining elements of romance and suspense with strong modern-day heroes and heroines. She currently resides in the Pacific Northwest with her author husband, Jack Davenport, and an obnoxious YorkiePoo named Pepper who may or may not be an international spy.

Like Piper's FB page and get to know her!
(www.facebook.com/piperdavenport)

* * *

USA Today Bestselling Author Jack Davenport is a true romantic at heart, but he has a rebel's soul. His writing is passionate, energetic, and often fueled by his true life, fiery romance with author wife, Piper Davenport. Twenty-five years as a professional musician lends a unique perspective into the world of rock stars, while his outlaw upbringing gives an authenticity to his MC series.

Like Jack's FB page and get to know him!
(www.facebook.com/JackDavenportAuthor)

www.ingramcontent.com/pod-product-compliance
Lightning Source LLC
Chambersburg PA
CBHW060439310726
48977CB00001B/256